Lucinda knew that she needed to do something.

Say something, maybe even shut the door.

But Josh had just short-circuited her brain.

"I have Thai," he said, leaning back but not stepping clear. "A bottle of California chardonnay, and some ice cream from this new place I've heard of—Calhoun Creamery?" He winked at her. "I hope it's good. I got you mint chocolate chip."

He kissed her. He remembered what her favorite kind of ice cream was.

And, more than any of that, he was here.

Josh was still standing over her, smiling down as if he was enjoying her complete and total befuddlement. "I'll just put this in the kitchen, shall I?"

"Oh. Yes." She gestured in the general direction of her kitchen and managed to get her door shut. She was suddenly very aware of why, exactly, having Josh at her place made her so twitchy.

It was because they were alone.

* * *

Claimed by the Cowboy is part of
the Dynasties: The Newports series—Passion and
chaos consume a Chicago real estate empire.

Dear Reader,

Welcome to Chicago! I lived in Chicago for almost six years. Although it's been over ten years since we left the Windy City, going back to Chicago was very much a literary homecoming for me, just like it was for Josh Calhoun.

Josh went to Chicago, fell in love and got married. But that life fell apart and he returned to the family's dairy business in Iowa. Now he's back for the first time in years to help out his friends, the Newports.

The last person he expects to run into is Lucy Wilde. Lucy had dated his best friend before the poor guy died of cancer and Josh and Lucy had a falling-out at the funeral. Dr. Lucinda Wilde is the preeminent cancer specialist in Chicago and in charge of Sutton Winchester's health. When she sees Josh, Lucy's reminded of everything she gave up back in school. She's not sure she can handle this blast from the past, but Josh refuses to give up on their friendship a second time.

Claimed by the Cowboy is a sensual story about fighting for your dreams and falling in love. I hope you enjoy reading this book as much as I enjoyed writing it. Look for other Dynasties stories for more about the Newports and the Winchesters! Be sure to stop by sarahmanderson.com and sign up for my newsletter at eepurl.com/nv39b to join me as I say, Long Live Cowboys!

Sarah

SARAH M. ANDERSON

CLAIMED BY THE COWBOY

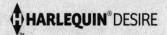

Special thanks and acknowledgment are given to Sarah M. Anderson for her contribution to the Dynasties: The Newports miniseries.

Recycling programs for this product may not exist in your area.

ISBN-13: 978-0-373-73483-2

Claimed by the Cowboy

Printed in U.S.A.

Sarah M. Anderson may live east of the Mississippi River, but her heart lies out West on the Great Plains. Sarah's book *A Man of Privilege* won an RT Reviewers' Choice Best Book Award in 2012.

Sarah spends her days having conversations with imaginary cowboys and American Indians. Find out more about Sarah's love of cowboys and Indians at sarahmanderson.com and sign up for the new-release newsletter at eepurl.com/nv39b.

Books by Sarah M. Anderson

Harlequin Desire

The Nanny Plan
His Forever Family

The Bolton Brothers

Straddling the Line
Bringing Home the Bachelor
Expecting a Bolton Baby

The Beaumont Heirs

Not the Boss's Baby
Tempted by a Cowboy
A Beaumont Christmas
His Son, Her Secret
Falling for Her Fake Fiancé

Texas Cattleman's Club: Lies and Lullabies

A Surprise for the Sheikh

Dynasties: The Newports

Claimed by the Cowboy

Visit her Author Profile page at Harlequin.com, or sarahmanderson.com, for more titles.

To Charles Griemsman, who occasionally lets me run completely wild with a story. Thank you for trusting me with your stories!

One

"May I help you?"

Josh Calhoun whipped off his Hollister-Whitney trucker hat and beamed a grin at the receptionist. "I sure hope so," he said, unconsciously letting his country accent bleed through a little more. He couldn't help it. This was the first time he'd been back in Chicago in five years and so much had changed.

Once, he'd tried to hide his accent. He'd tried to blend in with the big city.

Not anymore.

"I'm looking for the Newport boys," he went on, leaning his head toward the receptionist. Her eyes widened and he thought he saw a little bit of color come to her cheeks. He wasn't flirting—not intentionally—

but Sydney, God rest her soul, had said that this was just his way. His down-home charm was what had attracted her to him in the first place.

Damn it. He hadn't been in Chicago proper for more than thirty minutes and he was already thinking about Sydney again.

He hated this town.

"I'm Josh Calhoun," he went on. "They asked me to stop by."

Which was the only reason he had bothered to come back to Chicago. Brooks, Graham and Carson Newport were old college friends, and all three men had called him recently—apparently, without the others knowing that they were making the same call. Brooks Newport had asked for Josh's help in dealing with a rather stunning set of revelations about Sutton Winchester—Josh was still having trouble putting it all in order.

Apparently, Sutton Winchester was Carson's father and for a couple of months, Brooks and Graham had suspected that maybe the old real estate baron was their father, as well. But the paternity results had been conclusive—Brooks and Graham didn't share a father with Carson.

Ever since Sutton's involvement with their mother, Cynthia, had come to light, the Newport boys had been locked in a fierce battle with Sutton's daughters—Eve, Grace and Nora Winchester. As best Josh could gather from scrolling through the news stories on his phone, Sutton was on his deathbed.

The Winchester girls—particularly Eve—were not that happy to have a newly discovered brother who had strong opinions about staking his newfound inheritance claims. The rumors on the internet were flying fast and furious, and Josh had had trouble figuring out what was real and what were strategic PR leaks.

Brooks wanted Josh's legal advice on how to make Sutton pay for getting his mother pregnant with Carson and leaving her high and dry. His twin brother, Graham, wanted Josh's help in finding out who their father was, since it wasn't actually Sutton. And Carson, the baby of the family, desperately wanted Josh to come help calm Brooks down.

Josh wasn't sure he could actually do any of that. He was a former corporate lawyer and a dairy farmer. He negotiated with representatives and senators on legislation governing the dairy industry. He ran a multi-million-dollar dairy company. Sure, he had a reputation for being ruthless behind his good-time smile, but he wasn't a miracle worker.

Not for a single second did he think that anyone named Winchester would so much as give him the time of day. What did Chicago real-estate moguls care what a guy who made ice cream for a living thought? But he had to try. He owed the Newport boys.

The receptionist turned her attention to her computer screen. "Ah, yes. I see. Sadly, none of them are available." She looked up at Josh and he noticed that she had some dimples. "Brooks is in a private meeting and asked not to be disturbed. Graham is off-site, as is Carson."

"Off-site?" Chicago wasn't exactly a two-horse town. *Off-site* could mean anywhere. "Can you tell me where Graham and Carson are? They are expecting me." Irritation snaked up the back of his neck. At their request, he'd sucked it up and braved coming back to Chicago for the first time since the funeral, and they weren't even there to meet him?

The receptionist looked contrite. "I'm not at liberty to say where Graham is. However, Carson is on-site at the new children's hospital that the Newports are funding and constructing. I'd be happy to give you directions to the work site or…" She batted her eyelashes at him as her dimples deepened. "You're more than welcome to wait here."

Just as he had over the course of the last five years whenever a pretty lady made eyes at him, Josh did a gut check and waited to see if he'd have a reaction. Any reaction.

But there was nothing. Nothing other than the simple observation that this was a pretty girl who was flirting with him. He felt no attraction, no desire. There was absolutely no interest.

He ignored the black loneliness that existed in place of temptation and slapped on one of his best smiles. "I do need to speak with Carson," he said in his most apologetic tone. It wasn't the receptionist's fault that Josh was incapable of feeling anything.

The disappointment that crossed over her face was fleeting. "Let me get you those directions," she said in a much more professional tone.

"Thank you kindly," Josh said.

He was vastly out of his league and he knew it. He had vowed never to come back to Chicago, but there he was. The Newport boys were the only people on this earth who could've gotten him back inside city limits. They had been there for him at the hospital and at the funeral. In all likelihood, they'd probably saved his life. Not that Josh would ever tell anyone that, but when the people he cared for kept dying on him, it made it hard to put on a brave face and keep moving forward.

He was Josh Calhoun, heir to the Calhoun Creamery fortune and its current CEO. To the rest of the world, the fact that he had buried his parents and then his wife didn't matter as much as being one of the most powerful dairy owners in the country.

Well, it mattered to him. Sydney mattered to him. And when she'd been taken away from him, the Newport boys had been there.

Brooks, Graham and Carson mattered to him. It was the only reason he was in this godforsaken city, because if something happened to any of them, well, it just might be the end of the world. His world.

"Here you go," the receptionist said. It was a pity that Josh couldn't work up any attraction for her, but he just couldn't. "Shall I let Carson know that you're on your way?"

"Much obliged," Josh said, settling his hat on his head. "It's been a while since I drove in the city—how long do you think it'll take me to get there?"

The receptionist turned her attention back to her computer. After a few keystrokes, she said, "At this time of day, it shouldn't take you more than forty minutes."

Josh didn't try to hide his groan. Back home in Cedar Point, Iowa, forty minutes would put him three towns over. Here, forty minutes on a good traffic day would take him all of three miles.

The dimples were back on the receptionist. "It could be worse—it's only two in the afternoon."

"I know." He touched the brim of his hat and headed back out to his truck. It stuck out like a sore thumb there, parked among the sleek Jaguars and shiny sports cars of all sorts. But he'd had his truck since high school. It'd outlasted college, marriage and his wife's death. He wasn't about to get a new vehicle to meet someone else's preconceived notions of what a multimillionaire business owner should drive.

Because, most days, Josh didn't feel like a multimillionaire business owner. Most days he was up by four checking on the cattle in the milking operations of the Calhoun Creamery farm. He got crap on his boots and broke a sweat nearly every day. The only break he got was times like now. He'd been on his way home from Washington, DC, after meeting with a lobbyist for the National Dairy Council about what regulations they wanted to see included in the FDA's new organic standards.

As the owner of one of the largest dairies in the country and the CEO of the Calhoun Creamery, Josh's word carried some weight in those discussions. It was the only time he left the dairy farm.

Sighing heavily, Josh fired up the old truck and merged back into the hell that was Chicago traffic. He hoped the Newport boys appreciated the sacrifices he was making. And he was thankful that the traffic was just bad enough that he had to really pay attention. People in Iowa did not run lights like they did in Chicago. There, when the light turned red, people stopped. Here, when the light turned red, people sped up. He almost got rear-ended three separate times because he couldn't make himself run the red.

Finally, the new children's hospital work site came into view. It didn't look much like a children's hospital at this point—half of the exterior didn't even have walls. Josh studied his directions and saw that the receptionist had made a note that he was to pull down a side street and park in the back. She was a good receptionist. He almost wished that he'd been able to feel something for her. If he was going to be stuck in Chicago, a little distraction could go a long way.

He parked in the construction zone and there, at least, his truck blended in a little better. Josh made himself a promise. He would only stay in Chicago as long as it took to help the Newport boys get some of their issues sorted out. The moment he stopped being useful, he was out of there.

He'd worked too damned hard for a sense of equilibrium after Sydney's death. He knew better than to tempt fate again, and he simply did not have the mental energy to let himself fall into another deep depression.

If it were anyone but the Newports, he wouldn't be there.

But he was already there. So he better get this over with.

"But you understand that he's not dead yet," Dr. Lucinda Wilde said, trying her very best to keep a grip on her temper. She rarely got mad at patients— it was a waste of time and emotional energy. "I can only prolong his life if he stays in the hospital, under constant care. You do see that?"

Carson Newport stood to the doctor's left, his hands on his hips and a determined set to his eyes. On the doctor's right, Eve Winchester was glaring at Lucinda, her arms crossed and her brow furrowed with anger. All around them, the sounds of construction filled the air—as did dust. So much dust. She was going to have to shower before she went on her rounds again.

Lucinda had to hope that the construction materials being used here at the new children's hospital weren't carcinogenic. She vastly preferred her own hospital, where everything was already hospital-sterile. And she was not happy about having to leave her patients to trek halfway across town to mediate yet another dispute between the Newports and the Winchesters about her patient, Sutton Winchester.

Lucinda sighed and pushed her glasses back up her nose. She would have a better chance convincing a pack of wild dogs than Sutton Winchester's children that the scion of the Winchester fortune needed to stay in the hospital.

Never in her nine years as a practicing oncologist had she run into such a stubborn set of relatives. She adored her job and Chicago, but days like these had her muttering "city folk" to herself and longing for the wide-open spaces of Cedar Point, Iowa. Even cows were more reasonable than this.

"I understand that you're not interested in doing your job," Eve Winchester said in a tight voice.

"There's no need to be rude," Carson Newport snapped. "The good doctor *is* doing her job. No one lives forever—especially not bitter old men."

Eve wheeled on Carson and most likely would have demolished him in a verbal barrage of slings and arrows, but a voice interrupted them. "What seems to be the trouble?"

Lucinda froze. Absolutely, completely *froze* as a voice out of her past floated up from out of nowhere and made her blood run hot and cold at the same time.

It couldn't be. It simply wasn't possible that she'd heard *him*. Not after all this time. Not right now, when she was barely keeping herself together in the face of one of her most challenging cases yet.

But then Carson turned and said, "Josh!"

And a little bit of Lucinda died because she wasn't imagining this. She couldn't be. Josh Calhoun himself had walked out of her nightmares and into her line of sight.

Oh, God. Her breath caught in her throat as Josh approached. He looked exactly the same as he had the last time she'd seen him. He was wearing jeans and a red plaid shirt. His longish brown hair stuck out around the base of his ratty-looking ball cap that looked exactly like the one he'd worn every single day back in school.

No, no, *no.* This wasn't happening. It couldn't be.

Josh Calhoun—a ghost from her past that she never wanted to face again—smiled widely at their small group.

Until his gaze landed on her.

Lucinda wasn't surprised when that good-time grin of his died on the vine. After all, they hadn't exactly parted on the best of terms when Lucinda had made an absolute fool of herself on the worst day of her life and Josh had turned her down flat.

They stared at each other and Lucinda was at least a little relieved that he was just as surprised to see her as she was to see him.

And then everything got worse. Because Josh Calhoun, the boy who'd shattered her already broken heart, lifted one corner of his mouth in what she knew all too well was his real smile.

Oh. Oh, my. Something about him had changed. He was a little taller and a heck of a lot more broad in the shoulders. His chin was sharper now and his eyes...

Josh Calhoun had grown up.

Lucinda did not allow herself to feel a rush of instant attraction. Lust had no place in her life. It was an inconvenient emotion at best, and she only had so much emotional energy to spare after spending her days as the head of the oncology department at Midwest Regional Medical Center. She couldn't waste a bit of it, certainly not on the likes of Josh Calhoun, the last person she had allowed herself to lust over.

But watching Josh's lips curve into that real smile instead of the big one he used when he was befriending every single person in the room? Lust hit her low and hard, and she wasn't ready for it. She wasn't ready for him. Not now, not ever.

But she refused to let any of that show. She didn't suck in air, even though her lungs were burning. She didn't allow her skin and circulatory system to betray her in any way. She didn't even bat a single eyelash at him.

He was nothing to her. She didn't need him; she didn't want him, and she'd be damned if she let him know how much he'd hurt her back in high school.

Carson's scowl broke into a wide smile as he said, "You made it!" Then he and Josh wrapped their arms around each other and performed a few manly thumps on each other's back.

Lucinda couldn't help but glance at Eve during this display of masculine affection. Eve was rolling her eyes.

"Man, I'm glad to see you," Carson said to Josh. "Josh, this is Eve Winchester—it turns out that she's my sister."

"Stop telling people that," Eve snapped.

Lucinda sighed heavily. She'd heard variations on this particular theme over and over again whenever it came time to make a decision about Sutton Winchester's care. The Winchester daughters—Nora, Eve and Grace—refused to acknowledge that Carson was their half brother and did everything within their power to make sure that he did not have any say in family decisions.

But Carson Newport wasn't exactly taking this decision lying down.

Just as he did every time Eve threw this insult in his face, Carson opened his mouth to retort that she didn't have any choice in the situation. Lucinda knew the script by heart.

Josh didn't. Instead, he cut Carson off with a warm smile and an extended hand. "Ms. Winchester, it's a pleasure to make your acquaintance. I'm sorry that we can't meet under better circumstances, but Carson has told me how impressed he is with how you've been handling all the new developments."

Lucinda had no idea if this was a true statement

or not. Maybe it didn't matter. Josh's words went off like a little bomb in the conversation, completely resetting the discourse.

She shouldn't be surprised. Josh Calhoun had always been the peacemaker of their high school. He had a way of finding the common ground and making everyone happy.

Everyone except her.

"He...what?" Eve stared down at Josh's outstretched hand. "Who *are* you?"

If Josh was insulted by this lack of manners, he didn't show it. "Beg your pardon—I'm Josh Calhoun, of the Calhoun Creamery. I went to college with the Newport boys and I count them as some of my oldest friends. I understand that things have been challenging recently and I wanted to stop by and see if I could do anything to help." As he said this last bit, his gaze shifted back to Lucinda.

Oh, come on—was he seriously including *her* in that statement? If that's what he thought, he had another think coming.

But he was the Newports' oldest friend? Figured. As if the Winchester/Newport feud wasn't enough of a tangled web to be caught in, Josh Calhoun had to go and add another thread. A big, fat, *complicated* thread.

Carson jumped in, taking advantage of Eve's stunned silence. "Josh, this is Dr. Lucinda Wilde. She's the oncologist who's overseeing Sutton's care. If there's one thing that Eve and I can agree on..."

At this, Eve snorted. "It's that Dr. Wilde has managed to stabilize our father. Without her, he would probably already be dead."

"Dr. Lucinda Wilde," Josh said, rolling each of the words off his tongue as if he was trying to figure out which part was the strangest. He leaned forward, his hand out. "Lucinda? And you're an oncologist now? I should have guessed."

She did not want to touch him. So she nodded her head and stuck her hands behind her back. "Josh. Sorry," she added in a not-sorry voice. "Germs, you know."

Eve and Carson shared a look. "Do you two know each other?" Carson asked.

She didn't answer. She didn't want to cop to knowing Josh. She didn't want anyone in Chicago to know about their tangled past, and she absolutely didn't want to be thinking about Josh Calhoun, past or present.

Sadly, it seemed as though she didn't have much of a choice. "Yeah," Josh said, letting his hand hang out there for a second before he lowered it back to his side. "Well, I knew Lucy Wilde."

She shuddered at the sound of her name. She'd left Lucy Wilde behind when she'd left Iowa, and there was no going back. "We went to the same high school," she explained to Carson and Eve. "But only for two years." She shot a warning glare at Josh because if he took it upon himself to add to that simple truth, she might have to kick him somewhere very important.

He notched an eyebrow at her and something in his eyes changed, and she knew—*knew*—that he remembered exactly how things had gone down between them. Or not gone down, as the case may be. But, thankfully, all he said was "Yup."

"I'm very happy for the high school reunion, but none of this brings us any closer to getting my father out of the hospital," Eve Winchester snapped.

Josh—without looking away from her—asked, "Is that a possibility?"

Right. Lucinda had a purpose here that had nothing to do with Josh Calhoun or Lucy Wilde. She had ventured out to this dusty, half-finished work site to try to talk some sense into Carson and Eve because they were the most invested players in this family drama.

Not that that was saying a lot.

"It would be best for the patient if he remained in the oncology ward at Midwest," Lucinda said as all three looked at her. "I want to keep him under my direct supervision, and there are several experimental treatments I would like to try—with his consent— that have the potential to increase his life expectancy. There are promising developments with low-dose naltrexone…"

"I don't understand why these experimental treatments have to be done in the hospital," Eve snapped, cutting Lucinda off. "Every day that he's in a public space—and no, you can't promise me that his privacy will be respected in that hospital—it becomes that much more likely that *someone* will access his records, take pictures of him while he's incapacitated or bribe a nurse for information they can use against him in the court of public opinion." She paused and shot daggers at Carson. "I want him home where I know that he'll be protected and safe."

Ah, so they were back on the script again. Josh looked to Lucinda for a reply, but she was unable to provide any other details of her patient's medical condition to him. She was not about to break her Hippocratic oath for him.

Instead, it was Carson who answered. "We've been over this, Eve. He's sick. He belongs in a hospital." He turned to Josh. "He's got inoperable lung cancer—years of smoking and hard living, I guess. It's spread to his lymph nodes. Stage three."

Josh had the decency to wince.

"But," Eve said as she jumped back in, "he's not going to die tomorrow."

"You can't just cut the cancer out?" Josh asked Lucinda.

She glared at him even harder. "I cannot share anything about my patient's condition with a non-family member."

Carson rolled his eyes at her. "As Dr. Wilde has explained to us, due to the original tumor's location, she can't perform surgery and traditional chemo, and radiation won't be powerful enough to eradicate the malignant cells that have spread to the lymph system."

Josh turned to Eve. "I'm so sorry to hear this," he said in a gentle voice. "This must be hard for you and your sisters."

Eve appeared stunned by this olive branch—and Lucinda appreciated someone short-circuiting the bickering.

Josh Calhoun was the same as he'd always been, that much was clear. This was what he did. She'd seen him talk down two guys in the middle of a fight so that, within minutes, they were all sharing a soda and laughing about good times or whatever it was men laughed about while one was wiping the other's blood off his knuckles.

Once, she'd admired him for that. Okay, honestly— she'd more than admired him. She'd been fascinated by him. She'd never been much to look at, but Josh had never treated her like the know-it-all nerd everyone else did.

Well, almost everyone else. Josh's best friend in high school, Gary, had asked her out after she'd verbally smacked down some bullies who were mocking Gary for being unable to lift his own backpack after a chemo treatment. And since no one else had ever even remotely looked at Lucy Wilde as someone they might like to go see a movie with—much less kiss—she'd said yes.

Lucinda shook her head out of the past. How long had it been since she'd allowed herself to think of

Gary—or Josh? Years. It hadn't been that hard. She'd been busy with her medical career and dealing with the likes of the Winchesters and Newports. And the Winchesters and Newports took all of her attention.

She had, of course, expressed her concerns to Sutton's family—that was part and parcel of her job. She cared not only for her patients but their loved ones, as well. She'd had decades of helping people live and die—long before she'd become a doctor.

Long before she'd humiliated herself in front of Josh Calhoun.

But now that she thought of it, she couldn't remember witnessing anyone else expressing their sympathies to any of the Winchester daughters. Certainly not Brooks Newport or his brothers. Carson's grim acceptance of the situation had, until this moment, been as good as it got.

"Thank you," Eve replied quietly. Then she turned her attention to Carson. "I'm not giving up on him. I just want what's best for him and I don't think being in the hospital is it."

"What are the options?" Josh asked.

Why did he have to be here? Why did he have to be forging a peace between Eve and Carson?

Why did he have to be reminding her of things she'd tried so desperately to forget?

It was Carson who answered for her. "Eve and her sisters—*our* sisters—think it would be best to take him home. I'm not comfortable pulling him out of the hospital." He stared at Eve. "*We* have questions and I want him to live long enough to get some answers out of him."

It was blisteringly clear who the "we" was—Carson and his brothers.

Lucinda wanted to massage her throbbing temples.

Eve glared at him. "What you think doesn't matter. He's not really your father. You don't know him and you don't love him like I do—like *my sisters* do." Her gaze swung back to Lucinda and she looked more determined than ever, which was saying something. "Money is no object. I can have a private medical facility that meets your specifications set up at his estate in a matter of days. I want him out of the hospital and safely at home. And if you won't help move him," she threatened, "I will find a doctor who can."

"Beg your pardon," Josh interrupted in that gentle tone that Lucinda didn't really appreciate. "Does he *want* to stay in the hospital?"

It was a deceptively simple question and Lucinda knew it. What Sutton Winchester wanted was to go home and pretend he was not on death's door. He never wanted to see her face or the inside of a hospital ever again. But that was not what was best for him.

"Of course, he doesn't," Eve stated flatly.

"Because if he's got the means to be treated at home, maybe that would be best for everyone," Josh said as if this were the obvious conclusion instead of a solution that entailed an unnecessary health risk.

Well, that went sideways on her. Lucinda gave him a dull look and Carson was none too pleased at this announcement.

Undaunted by their open hostility, Josh went on, "Carson, you've got to realize that if he's more comfortable, he'll likely be willing to answer some of those questions, don't you think?"

She wanted to strangle him. It was bad enough that he was here and worse that she was having to talk to him. But for him to come down on the wrong side?

That, however, wasn't the worst of it. No, what was the worst was that she could see Carson start to waver. Damn it. She knew there were many unanswered questions and she also knew that, currently, Sutton was in no mood to unburden his soul.

Carson Newport had been her ally in keeping Sutton Winchester in the hospital. But, before her eyes, she could see him switch sides. "Well…"

Josh didn't wait for Carson to talk himself out of it. "If it won't compromise his care, that is." He turned his attention to Lucinda and turned on his all-American charm. "If Eve can get the room set up to your specifications, would you be willing to release Mr. Winchester? I know that no one wants to risk his health. That has to come first. I think we can all agree that your word is final, can't we?" He glanced around their small circle, gathering approval to him like a cloak.

Lucinda blinked at him. Was that the bone he was

going to throw her—that she had the final word? Very neatly, Josh Calhoun had sidestepped, diffused or completely undercut weeks of bitter arguments— and boxed her into a corner.

What she wanted to say was that he was out of his ever-loving mind and he could go crawl back into whatever hole he'd crawled out of.

But she didn't. She had a professional reputation to maintain, and she would be damned if she let Josh Calhoun take that away from her, too. "In no way would moving him at this stage of his treatment be a good idea," she said firmly.

This fell on deaf ears. "Okay," Carson announced. "If we can get a room set up in his home, we can move him. But our brothers aren't going to like this."

"Graham and Brooks are absolutely *not* my brothers," Eve said just as her phone buzzed. She glanced at it and Lucinda saw a small smile break through her icy demeanor. "Dr. Wilde, if you could get a list of equipment we'll need, I'll have everything else taken care of."

"You do understand that this will be very expensive, don't you?" Lucinda tried a last-ditch attempt. "You'll need twenty-four-hour care to monitor him, as well—and not some random home-health nurse. He needs oncology specialists around him at all time."

Eve and Carson shared a look. "That's fine," Eve said with a smile that made Lucinda's blood run cold. "There's plenty of room at the house. I'll have the

guest quarters prepared for your stay. Hire whomever you need."

"Ms. Winchester!" Lucinda gaped at her in shock.
When had she lost complete and total control?

Josh cleared his throat. *Oh, yeah.* The moment
he'd walked back into her life.

But she didn't get any further than that. Carson
stepped forward and said, "That sounds like a good
idea to me. Would you be able to do that, Dr. Wilde?"

This simply could not get worse. She had already
been dragged into more than enough Winchester/
Newport drama. Personally supervising Sutton Winchester's care at home would only double and then
triple that.

She had opened her mouth to find the words to
politely yet firmly refuse when Josh spoke up. "At
the very least," he said, shooting her one of his big
smiles that did absolutely nothing to her, "would you
be able to see him settled?"

"I'm the head of the oncology department at Midwest," she told him with an edge to her voice. "I
cannot simply disappear to a private home for days
or what could even turn out to be weeks at a time."

Carson gave her a smile that bordered on preda-
tory. "I'm sure, for an appropriate donation to that
new cancer pavilion expansion they've been planning, they'll be more than happy to help you find a
way to make this work into your schedule."

In other words, her medical services were going to
the highest bidder—and there were no bidders higher

in the greater Chicago region than the Winchesters and the Newports. The Newports were already funding this new children's hospital. In the grand scheme of things, the cost of an expanded cancer pavilion meant nothing to them or the Winchesters.

Lucinda *absolutely* did not want to be a pawn in this tug-of-war between the two families, but that pavilion would do a lot of good for a lot of people. Damn it all to hell. "I suppose I could move a few appointments around and take a couple of days. But I won't compromise anyone else's care. And if I don't believe your father will receive excellent care at home, I won't allow him to be discharged."

Eve sniffed, and there was determination in her voice as she said, "Fine. Do whatever you have to do. I'll have the guest quarters set up." Abruptly, she turned away and began texting rapidly.

Lucinda sighed. She turned to Carson—and Josh. "I just want what's best for my patient," she reminded the men.

"It sounds like *you're* what's best for the patient," Josh said as if he were seriously complimenting her.

Lucinda had never physically assaulted anyone in her entire life, but she was damned close to taking a swing at Josh. That did it. He needed to get his nose out of this medical situation—and her business— before she lost what was left of her temper. "Can I talk to you for a second?" she demanded, not bothering to smooth her tone over with a smile.

Carson's eyebrows jumped up, but Josh showed no sign that he understood the danger. "Sure."

Good. Great. She was going to tell Josh Calhoun off the way she should have done seventeen years ago, and then she was going to get on with her life.

Without him.

Two

Josh stood there for a moment in a state of total shock. His mind had to be playing tricks on him. *Chicago* had to be playing tricks on him. Because there was just no reasonable explanation for why he was here with Lucy Wilde. He stared after her as she stalked away.

"I take it you two aren't the best of friends," Carson commented drily as he watched Josh watch Lucy.

"Probably safe to say that," Josh admitted. But once, they had been. Lucy and Gary and Josh. Three peas in a pod, his grandpa had always said. Until it'd just been the two of them. And then Josh had done what had been the hardest thing he'd done in his life—say no to Lucy Wilde.

Carson pondered Josh's statement. "Old girl-friend?"

"No, nothing like that." Which was not entirely the truth, but Josh got the feeling that Lucy might personally tear him limb from limb if he gave anyone any indication of how close they'd been once. "Can you give me a few minutes?"

A grin twisted Carson's lips. "Given how she was trying to kill you with looks alone, you might need more than a few minutes."

"I didn't come here for her," Josh said in as good-natured a tone as he could manage. "Let me get this settled, and then we can go somewhere and get a beer and you can fill me in on what the hell has been happening around here." As if he could just "settle" the matter of Lucy when she was clearly out for blood.

Carson looked defeated. "That's going to take a lot more than one beer," he said. "Go on. Another five minutes isn't going to change anything."

"Thanks." Josh took a deep breath and began to follow Lucy Wilde.

Except she wasn't Lucy, not anymore. Lucy had been a wide-eyed, freckled girl who had been wildly in love with his best friend, Gary Everly. Josh had actually liked her—he'd liked her quite a bit. She'd had a dry sense of humor and a sharp wit that she only used when people had her backed into a corner, which they did at their own risk. She'd been smart—smarter than either of the boys.

And she'd loved Gary. It hadn't mattered that he'd

been sick. More times than he could count, Josh had caught Lucy gazing at Gary with unabashed adoration. It had never bothered him. Really. Lucy had been one of the best things to happen to Gary, and Josh had not begrudged his childhood friend the little bit of happiness Lucy was able to bring him in a dark time.

Josh had tried to make Gary happy, too. Minigolf, cow tipping, the movies—together, they'd made a hell of a group, tearing up Cedar Point, Iowa. He'd had the car and the Calhoun cash; Gary had had his bucket list; and Lucy had kept them from doing anything truly stupid. In fact, if Josh was remembering things correctly, it'd been Lucy who'd passed judgment on whomever Josh had dated. A lot of the time, they'd been a foursome.

But a lot of the time…it'd just been the three of them. Him, her and Gary.

Until Gary had died. Four days before his eighteenth birthday. Of leukemia. Because his folks hadn't been able to afford to bring him to Chicago or anyplace that had a really good oncology department.

Not that it would have mattered. After all, Sydney had had access to the best medical care in the country and it hadn't been enough to save her.

Josh was already clinging to his sanity by his fingernails just being back in Chicago, but to suddenly find himself confronted with Lucy Wilde and Gary's memory was almost too much. He wanted to bail and go back to his cows and stay far away from the people he loved because that was the best way of keeping them safe.

He did not want Lucy Wilde to remind him of yet another person he'd lost.

Not that he had a lot of choice in the matter. He walked toward her slowly so that he could try to put his thoughts in order. This was not the same girl he remembered. Oh, sure, she still had on a massive pair of eyeglasses that gave her an owlish appearance. And the only thing that seemed to have changed about her stick-straight blond hair was that she had pulled it up into a bun. But half of her hair had worked itself free and fell around her face and shoulders, making her look ethereal.

Josh almost smiled. Lucy had never had a head for fashion or style and, given that she was wearing a shapeless doctor's coat over equally shapeless black trousers and a mannish blue button-up blouse, that hadn't changed, either.

But the fire in her eyes? That was something new. Something that had made him come to a screeching halt and stare at her in openmouthed wonder.

The way he had the last time he'd seen her.

She reached her destination and spun, glaring at him. Her toe began to tap and he wouldn't have been surprised if she'd pulled out a phone and checked the time.

"It's good to see you again, Lucy," he began.

He didn't get any further than that. "What are

you doing here?" At least she kept her voice to a fierce whisper.

"Like I said, I'm friends with the Newport boys. They called me and asked for help sorting out this mess."

"Don't give me that," she snapped. "Because rolling up here and turning on all of your charm to convince my patient's family that he would be best served outside the hospital is not exactly how I wanted to see you again, Joshua Calhoun."

Ouch. She was busting out the *Joshua* already. So much for warm, fuzzy reunions. But he couldn't help himself. Teasing Lucy had been so much fun because she always gave so much better than she got. He heard himself slipping right back into it. "So, how did you want to see me again?"

If looks could kill, he would probably need emergency medical help right now. "I didn't."

There wasn't a single thing about this situation that should make him smile, but he did. "I'm just going to go out on a limb here, but you seem upset with me."

Her eyes widened at the challenge. "Oh? Do you think? No. You obviously don't. Because if you did think, you would remember…" Abruptly, her voice trailed off into a new emotional place, replacing the anger that flamed out all over her face.

It almost looked painful.

He didn't like that pained look. Because he did remember. He remembered quite clearly. What had happened between them—it wasn't the sort of thing a man forgot. He may not think about it every single day of his life. But, no, he hadn't forgotten about going to Gary's funeral and Lucy clinging to his hand the whole time and then pulling him out back at the wake and telling him that she needed him, needed him so badly because she hurt so much and she just wanted to not hurt and would he…

"Oh, my God," Lucy gasped, recoiling in horror. "Stop. Stop right there."

Josh shook himself. He was pretty sure he hadn't said anything out loud. "What?"

"Don't." Somehow her eyes got even wider and, behind her thick glasses, even more owlish. Her back straightened and he realized that, despite the fact that she was wearing an almost sexless doctor's uniform, she wasn't the same girl he remembered. She was taller and, with her shoulders squared, he could see that a woman's curves filled out her body.

If she'd had those curves back then…

"Don't what?" he asked, although he knew that was a lame dodge. She'd always been so incredibly perceptive, and as for him—well, he'd always been an open book. He'd only ever been able to hide one thing from her—exactly how much he'd liked her.

The only other woman he'd never been able to hide anything from was Sydney.

Which meant Lucy had realized exactly what he'd been thinking.

"Just don't, Josh," she finished weakly. Then, she

blushed. Hard. So hard that she went scarlet from the tips of her ears to the base of her neck. Lucy was so tomato red that he didn't even need to look at her hands to know they'd turned bright red, too.

"Lucy…"

But whatever vulnerability he'd glimpsed was gone in an instant. "Don't you dare 'Lucy' me," she interrupted. Everything about her body tightened as if she were fighting off some urge. He had no idea whether she was going to punch him or what. "I am Dr. Lucinda Wilde now, and so help me, Josh Calhoun, if you roll up in here and in any way, shape or form compromise the care of my patients, I will personally make sure the rest of your life is a living hell."

She spun on her heel and he knew she was done with him, but, damn it, he wasn't willing to let it go. He reached out and grabbed her hand. "Lucy, it doesn't have to be like this."

She froze. Her gaze dropped down to where he had her by the hand. Her skin was warm and soft against his, softer than he'd expected it to be. He closed his fingers around hers and, without really thinking about it, pulled her closer to him.

A feeling so unfamiliar, so foreign that he couldn't name it right away, hit him low in the gut. Lucy. This was Lucy, and against all odds he'd missed her. He took another step into her, closing the distance between them.

Dear God in heaven, what he was feeling right now? Desire. Want.

Need.

Josh Calhoun did a gut check and, for the first time in five years, his gut told him to go for it.

For Lucy Wilde, of all people.

His heart began to pound and his skin began to prickle. He inhaled deeply. She smelled of hospitals and antiseptics and, underneath that, a hint of something sweet, and all he wanted to do was lean his head down and taste her to find out what that sweetness was.

Then she looked up at him, her light blue eyes impossibly wide. "Yes, it does."

He wasn't going to accept that. "Have dinner with me."

That made her laugh—and pull her hand away from his grip. "Seriously? Am I not making myself clear? I thought you were smarter than this, Josh. I don't want to see you. We're not friends anymore."

"We are." Her eyeballs bugged out of her head at this declaration. "Well, we can be again."

"No," she said softly, turning away from him. This time he didn't try to stop her. "After what happened? No, we can't."

He watched her go, her words echoing louder in his head the farther away she got.

She hated him. Well, he supposed he deserved nothing less than her contempt. She'd needed him to comfort her after her high school sweetheart had died and he'd…

He'd forced himself to turn her down. He'd embarrassed her then and he'd embarrassed her again, that much was obvious. She only ever got that red when she lost her temper.

But she didn't realize how hard it'd been to say no to her. How much it'd hurt to know that he'd added to her pain. To have twice watched Lucy Wilde walk away from him and know that he'd screwed it up.

Damn it all to hell and back.

He watched a construction worker scurry out of Lucy's way right before she disappeared around a corner. He should let it go. She'd made her position more than clear. Just as she had seventeen years ago when he'd rejected her.

But it'd been different then. He'd been a kid in mourning for his best friend and due to leave Cedar Point in just a few weeks for college in Chicago. He'd rationalized that a clean break was best for all of them.

Now?

Now his gut was telling him that maybe it was okay to look at another woman and feel something. Something good. Something right.

He hadn't felt anything in so long…

No. He wasn't going to let Lucy Wilde walk away from him a second time with so much unsaid between them. He wasn't the same confused kid he'd been. He was a man now and he knew what he wanted.

He made his way back over to where Carson had been waiting for him, texting on his phone the whole time. With any luck, Carson hadn't been paying attention to his and Lucy's conversation.

"That seemed to go well," he said without looking up.

Josh sighed. One thing was abundantly clear.

His luck had run out.

Lucinda did her very best to ban all thoughts of Josh Calhoun from her mind as she moved through her afternoon. She'd spent more time at the children's hospital site than she'd meant to and was behind schedule. She hated being behind schedule. Things happened on time or there were dire consequences in her world. When it came to the health of her patients, waiting could be fatal.

This was what she kept telling herself as she moved around Midwest's oncology ward, her hair still damp from the quick shower she'd taken to wash the construction dust off. Like any other day, some people were making progress and some people were losing the battle. Mrs. Adamczak was sitting up in bed and smiling for the first time in weeks. Mr. Gadhavi, however, had not responded to treatment and, as hard as it would be, Lucinda was going to recommend that he be sent home for hospice.

This was where her focus needed to be—on the people she could still help. That did not include Gary Everly and it did not include Josh Calhoun.

It did, however, include Sutton Winchester.

It was madness that she was even going to consider allowing him to continue his treatment away from this hospital. If it were any other person in the entire city of Chicago, it wouldn't be an option. It wouldn't even be a figment of someone's imagination.

But Sutton Winchester wasn't any other person. And his children weren't going to let her forget it.

But before she could even get to his room, she was stopped by the vice president of Midwest, John Jackson, outside the nurses station on the oncology ward. "Dr. Wilde," Jackson said with an unnaturally bright look to his eyes. "Just the doctor I was looking for!"

Lucinda didn't have time for ego stroking right now. She knew that if Jackson worked up a proper head of steam, he could go on for hours. "How much money did they offer you?"

Jackson pulled up short and blinked at her. "How did you…"

"Because I'm not stupid, Mr. Jackson. I was there when Eve Winchester decided that this was going to be a reality whether I thought it was a good idea or not. You should merely count yourself lucky that you're going to get the money for the cancer pavilion expansion out of it, shouldn't you?"

Jackson didn't know her very well and it was clear that he didn't know how he was supposed to take this attitude. But he hadn't made it to being a vice president of a hospital without understanding how to cover his tracks. "Just think of all the people that we'll be able to help," he said, putting all available lipstick on this pig of a situation.

"Yes, yes—I know. I hope you at least negotiated for the entire cost of construction?"

"The Newports and the Winchesters have agreed to $250 million!" The man actually did a little dance. "I've never seen anything like it. Whatever you did, Dr. Wilde, do you think you could do it again? We could use a new cardiac cath lab, too."

She glared at him hard enough that he took a step backward. God, this whole situation had left her with a bad taste in her mouth. What else could go wrong today?

At that exact moment, the ward doors opened and a cart laden with floral arrangements was wheeled in. This was normally a happy time of her day as she got to see the flowers bring a bit of hope to people's eyes.

"As I said to Mr. Winchester's children, I will only allow him to be treated in his home if they can get a room set up to my specifications and if it won't compromise the treatment of my other patients," she told Jackson as she kept an eye on the beautiful arrangements being off-loaded. She shouldn't like the flowers. She never got any, and the last time anyone had actually given her flowers had been at her senior prom with Gary.

He'd only been able to stand for the photos and for one dance. He'd gotten her a corsage, though. And then he made Josh Calhoun dance with her several other times throughout the night.

The last bouquet on the cart was a small arrangement of sunflowers and daisies—bright and sunny and full of the promise of tomorrow. The delivery guy set the bouquet on the nurses station counter and Lucinda saw one of her favorite nurses, Elena, glance at the card. Elena's eyes got very wide very fast, and then she looked up at Lucinda and smiled.

Elena must have a new boyfriend. That was sweet of him to send flowers to work.

Lucinda turned her attention back to Mr. Jackson. "...find a way to make this work," he was saying in his best salesman tone.

Elena held the card out to another nurse, who read the name on it and started giggling. "Fine," she told Jackson. Because who was she? Just Sutton Winchester's doctor, that's all. Just the one person who wanted him to get the best treatment in the best place from the best people.

Apparently, that made her the bad guy there.

Well, she knew when it was time to cut her losses. You couldn't hold back the tides and you couldn't hold back Eve Winchester when she made up her mind about something.

Jackson was still making noises about pavilions, patients and money when Elena carried the sunny bouquet over to Lucinda. "It's for you," she said.

Lucinda wasn't offended by the nurse's awestruck tone. She didn't believe it, either. "Seriously?" She grabbed the card out of Elena's hand. Yes, that was her name on the envelope. Typed, not handwritten: "Dr. Lucinda Wilde."

"When will you have a list of things Mr. Winchester needs to get ready?" Jackson asked in a tone of voice that was one small step removed from a flat-out demand. "I don't want to keep Ms. Winchester or Mr. Newport waiting."

"Give me an hour," Lucinda all but growled at him. Elena was watching her with naked interest, Jackson wasn't leaving her alone about the Newports and the Winchesters, and she was holding in her hands a card from Josh Calhoun, because who else would send her flowers?

No one, that's who. She'd always been something of an introvert. She had a few good friends and it was more than enough for her.

Never in her entire life had she wanted to go hide more than she did right now.

"Great! I'll check back in an hour, okay?" For the love of everything holy, Jackson looked so much like an overeager golden retriever at this moment that Lucinda was tempted to dig a treat out of her pocket and throw it just to get him to go away.

"Yeah." She should probably work a little harder on sucking up to the hospital administrators, but she just didn't have it in her today.

Once Jackson was out of sight, Elena whispered, "Well?" and crowded closer to read the card over her shoulder.

Lucinda slipped the card into her pocket and grabbed the floral arrangement. There was no way in hell she was going to read it right now, with half of the nurses on duty pretending not to listen in. If she was going to turn beet red again, she wanted to do so in the privacy of her own closet. "It looks like I'm going to be picking up some extra shifts at a private residence. I'm going to need a few trusted nurses who can keep their mouths shut." The irony of the situation didn't escape her. She wasn't going to read Josh's note in front of them because she didn't trust a single one of them, but she was asking them to come to Winchester's estate and help her discreetly manage him there. "Are you interested?"

The difference was, of course, that patient privacy was the law and that law was drilled into them over and over again. Her personal life, however, was fair game and everyone knew it.

"Of course!" Elena's gaze darted over to Sutton's room. Yeah, everyone knew who they were talking about. "Any word on what it'll pay?"

"I'll make sure it's worth your while. Now, if you'll excuse me…" Lucinda juggled the flowers and her tablet and, randomly tapping on the screen to make it look as if she was doing something important instead of fleeing like a trapped rat, turned on her heel and started down the hallway.

She couldn't flee fast enough. "Is he cute?" Elena called after her. "Or she—it's fine with us either way."

As if Lucinda hadn't been put on the spot enough

already. She had always avoided the *Grey's Anatomy*–style hospital romances that seemed to permeate Midwest. And, yeah, on some level, she probably knew that people assumed she didn't date men because she was a lesbian or asexual.

But was it really such a common assumption that Elena would announce it in the middle of the hallway like that?

"Don't you need to check on Mrs. Adamczak?" Lucinda shot back over her shoulder as she walked through the wide swinging doors. Without giving Elena a chance to catch up, she hurried to her office and blissfully shut the door. It wasn't much of an office. Part of the plans for the expanded cancer pavilion was redesigning the doctors' offices to make patients feel more comfortable when they sat down for life-and-death discussions. Right now, Lucinda barely had enough room for a desk and two chairs. But she had a door and a lock, and that was all she needed right now.

She pulled the envelope out of her pocket and realized with horror that her hands were shaking. *No. No.* She was absolutely not going to let Josh Calhoun get to her again.

She slipped a small card out. "L—I will always be your friend. Let me take you out to dinner. J"

Below that was an Iowa phone number.

She had to stop thinking it couldn't get worse. Because at this point, fate was merely toying with her.

Three

"I might be stuck here for a couple of days," Josh told his grandfather, Peter Calhoun, who'd called just as Josh was getting into his truck after leaving Carson's place.

He wasn't sure what he hoped that his grandfather would say. Peter Calhoun was still the chairman of the Calhoun Creamery, although he was well into his eighties and little more than a figurehead at this point. For all intents and purposes, Josh ran the creamery as CEO. And he hated being away from it.

He almost wanted his grandfather to tell him to come home right now. To heck with the Newports and the Winchesters and the whole city. Chicago was not his town. And the longer he was there, the more everything would hurt.

But if he turned tail and ran—and there was no mistaking the fact that that was exactly what it would be—then what would they think of him? Brooks and Graham and Carson and, yes, Lucy?

He'd given up Lucy's friendship once without a fight. He could not willingly forfeit the Newports' friendship, too.

"No big rush," his grandfather said, his voice crackling with age. "You work too hard, son. Take all the time you need."

That was not exactly what Josh wanted to hear. "It'll only be a few more days," he said as if his grandfather had asked him to come home. "I think the Newport boys need me to be here long enough to see Sutton Winchester settled a little bit. I won't be here a moment longer."

There was a pause on the other end of the phone before his grandfather said, "Josh, I know it must be hard for you to be back in Chicago, but I'm serious. Your brothers and sisters are doing a great job holding down the fort. Take the time you need to take. The cows aren't going anywhere. Paige has the situation well in hand and Trevor is helping cover for you. You know, I think it's been good for him to have a little more responsibility."

Josh scowled, not that his grandfather could see it. He did his best to take care of his siblings.

"Unless there's something else bothering you?" Peter Calhoun asked tentatively.

"DC was fine," Josh quickly said. "I think we'll see some good things for the creamery in the new regulations. We should be able to capitalize on the push for hormone-free products and grow our market share." That wasn't what his grandfather had asked, but switching back into corporate-lawyer mode was almost automatic for him.

And they both knew it. "But…" the older man said in his gentle way.

Josh sighed. "You're not going to believe this," he said, pinching the bridge of his nose between his fingers. "But Lucy Wilde is Sutton Winchester's oncologist."

"Is that so?" At first Josh thought his grandfather didn't remember who Lucy was, but then he added, "Have you seen her since graduation?"

"No." Josh left it at that. He didn't need to tell his grandfather that Lucy had looked at him with absolute venom in her eyes, and he also didn't need to mention that he had sent her flowers already.

"An oncologist? Well, good for her. You know…" His grandfather trailed off and Josh could infer what the old man was not saying.

You know, we always wondered what happened between you two. You know, she was such a nice girl. You know, you know, you know.

Shortly after Lucy and Josh had gone to their respective colleges far, far away from each other, Lucy's folks had moved out of Cedar Point. The Wilde family had no more connections with Iowa that he knew of. Lucy had not come back.

But Josh had.

And he would again.

Josh knew he shouldn't be sending flowers to anyone. What he had was his job and his family. And that was all he needed. He didn't need the feeling of desire that hit him low in the gut. He'd lived a good five years without it, after all.

And he especially didn't need to feel that desire for someone he had a messy history with. The less complicated his life, the happier he was.

And one thing was blindingly obvious—Lucy Wilde was complicated. With a capital *C*.

"If you see her again, you tell her I said hi," his grandfather went on as if Josh were actively participating in this conversation. "You know, she was such a nice girl. I'm glad to hear she is doing well. And Josh?"

"Yeah?"

"There's no rush. If you need to take a couple of weeks in Chicago, that's fine. Your brother and sisters and I have everything under control."

If Josh didn't know any better, he'd think his grandfather was actively telling him *not* to come home. "Yeah, okay. I'll let you know." And with that he hung up.

He stared at his phone. Why did his grandfather's insistence that he take some time off bother him so much? Josh didn't need to take time off. He was fine. He'd been fine for a long time.

His mind called up the images of the three women he'd had conversations with today—the Newports' receptionist, Eve Winchester and Lucy Wilde. He hadn't responded to Eve at all, but that feeling had been mutual. Nothing unusual there.

But that receptionist…she'd been actively flirting with Josh. He'd felt nothing other than noting she was a pretty girl. No reaction, no interest. As usual.

Then he'd come around that corner and seen Lucy. That had inspired a reaction in him, which was putting it mildly. Was it just the shock of seeing her again after all these years? Or was it something else?

Before he could fire up the truck, his phone buzzed and lit up with a text message. Josh jolted and almost dropped his phone, but he managed to keep a grip on it and prevent it from sliding down between his thigh and the seat.

For Pete's sake. His heart thumping along at a good clip, he looked at the screen. It was a Chicago area code. The text message read, I don't know if dinner is such a good idea.

Oh, thank God. Lucy had gotten the flowers. And she had not promptly told him to go to hell. On the whole, that was an improvement from their earlier conversation and, for some reason, made him feel… hopeful?

Why? Don't you eat dinner?

The little bubble popped up on the screen that meant she was typing something back. What do you really want?

The hell of it was, he didn't actually know. Why wasn't he letting this drop? Was it simply because he was in Chicago and it was easier to think about Lucy than it was to think about Sydney? Or was it because he wasn't sure what he was supposed to do to help out the Newport boys and this problem seemed less challenging?

Or…was it something else?

His fingers curved and he could almost feel her hand in his again, see the way her eyes had widened when he'd pulled her in.

It didn't seem possible that he wanted her. Not after five years without a single damned spark of attraction to any woman.

So he sidestepped the unfamiliar emotions and focused on what he could handle. To catch up with an old friend, he texted back.

The little bubble popped up, went away and then popped up again before he got a reply. You shouldn't send me flowers at work.

I didn't have your home address. It's just dinner, Lucy. He almost added, I've missed you, but at the last second, he changed his mind and backspaced over the words. Except he hit the wrong button and accidentally sent a partial text that read, I've mp.

Crap.

Sorry, he quickly texted. Hit the wrong button.

She didn't answer for the longest time—so long, in fact, that Josh was pretty sure she had decided to call it a day.

Then her reply popped up. One dinner. That's it.

Tonight? The moment he hit Send, he felt stupid. He hadn't come to Chicago for Lucy. He'd told Carson as much. He was here for the Newport boys and nothing more. Tonight was about settling in with a couple of six-packs and doing his level best to keep Brooks from going off the deep end.

But suddenly he realized he wanted her to come to dinner with him. And not just because they were old friends. Okay, because they were old friends— the very best of old friends.

Hell. He didn't know why he needed her to say yes. Only that he did.

Can't. Dealing with the Winchesters.

Disappointment unfurled in his chest, but then another text popped up. Tomorrow night. Meet me at Lou Malnati's on N. State. 7 o'clock.

Chicago pizza? I'm there, he texted.

All this was, he told himself, was two old friends getting together for dinner at a classic Chicago restaurant. And Josh would be lying if he said he didn't miss Chicago food. Cedar Point, Iowa, was a great small town and a wonderful place to grow up, but folks there considered Applebee's to be fancy and the ethnic food section of the grocery store consisted of refried beans and tortilla chips. Chicago dining was one of the very few things that he missed about the city.

His stomach rumbled.

So that was why he was suddenly excited. Not the fact that Lucy had said yes, but that he was going to get a good Chicago pizza for the first time in a long time.

Nothing more.

This was a mistake. Lucinda had spent the last twenty-four hours doing her regular job and dealing with the Winchester sisters. She understood that they loved their father, and she also understood that they only wanted what was best for him.

But they were going to drive her past madness in record time.

And what she wanted right now more than anything was to be curled up on her couch with a pint of ice cream—yes, Calhoun Creamery ice cream—and watching a Sandra Bullock movie.

She did not want to be walking into a pizzeria at 6:58 on a Thursday night. And she most especially did not want to be meeting Josh Calhoun.

Somehow, though, that hadn't stopped her from rushing home after work to change. Even worse, it hadn't stopped her from putting on one of her few dresses, a sleeveless navy blue wrap dress that she had worn to weddings and funerals alike. The evening was cool, and she'd put on a cream-colored cardigan so she didn't feel naked.

She knew that if the people from work saw her—especially someone like Elena—they would lose their collective minds, because Lucinda never dressed up, never put on mascara and lipstick, and she never, ever wore her hair down. All the things she was doing right now.

There was only one explanation. She had lost what was left of her mind.

This is not a date, she told herself as she forced her feet to carry her through the door and into the restaurant. This was two old friends catching up—nothing more, nothing less.

Which did nothing to explain the way her stomach fluttered when Josh caught sight of her and stood up. Now that she was braced for seeing him again, it was easier to see how he had changed compared with what she remembered. He was taller and broader—a fact that was only emphasized by the heather-gray blazer he wore over a white dress shirt. He didn't have on his trademark hat, either. His hair was neatly combed and he was clean-shaven.

Two thoughts hit Lucinda at the exact same time.

God, he was the most handsome man she'd ever seen. So much more than the cute boy she'd been friends with.

And oh, *hell*. This was a date.

Those two things were quickly followed by a

third, even more terrifying thought—it was too late to back out now.

"Lucy!" Josh came around the table and made a move as though he was going to hug her, but then he pulled up short and instead just put his hands on her shoulders. "You look great," he said.

It was the kind of thing that he could've just tossed off as a social nicety. But his gaze traveled over her body—which made her want to curl up self-consciously into a small ball and hide. This was painful. Excruciatingly so. She knew she was a failure when it came to sensuality. Heck, wasn't that why she'd put on the cardigan? Because it hid her shapeless body—and it was as close to her lab coat as she could get away with outside the hospital?

Then he added, "Wow. You've really grown up," in a tone that was uncomfortably close to reverential.

Was that a compliment? It had to be. There was no mocking eye roll, no barely contained snicker behind his words. And, truthfully, she was pretty sure she'd be able to tell. She'd always been able to read Josh better than his own mother.

No, he was being sincere. And that somehow made everything worse. Lucinda forced herself to smile. "So have you. I'm surprised to see that hat isn't chemically bonded to your head."

"Hey!" Josh yelped in mock embarrassment. "At least I stopped sleeping with it on."

Against her will, Lucinda laughed. "Maturity in action, huh?"

Josh tried to look sheepish and didn't quite manage it. "Here," he said, stepping to the side and pulling out her chair for her. "Let me get this for you."

Yeah, this was a date. Back when they'd been friends in high school, Josh had treated her exactly the way he'd treated Gary—no special favors, no coddling. And certainly no holding chairs for either of them.

Her heart began to pound wildly as she sat. What was she doing? She didn't date. She didn't go out. She worked and she slept, and that was it. If this really was a date—and all signs seemed to be pointing to it—she had no idea what she was supposed to do or when she was supposed to do it without making a total fool of herself.

All she knew was that she was not going to make a fool out of herself. Not again.

Josh crossed to the other side of the table and sat down. "I don't know about you," he said in a light tone, "but I spent all day dealing with the Newport boys. I need a beer."

Okay, she could do this. As long as she didn't throw herself at him again, this would be fine. "And I was handling the Winchester girls," she admitted. That information didn't violate the HIPAA privacy laws, especially not when Josh already knew what was going on.

And a beer was exactly what she needed right now to get through this evening, too.

"What can I get you folks tonight?" a perky young waitress asked.

"I've missed Chicago deep-dish pizza like you wouldn't believe," Josh said, looking at her. "Is it okay if we get one to share?"

"That's fine." Lucinda also ordered a salad and Goose Island pale ale, while Josh ordered a Percheron Draft Stout ale.

Once the waitress left, Lucinda decided to go on the offensive. "Okay, so explain to me how you know the Newport boys, as you call them, and why you miss Chicago deep-dish pizza." Because if she could get Josh talking about himself, he wouldn't ask questions about her, and he especially wouldn't do something horrific like apologize for what happened all those years ago.

Josh gave her a look and she got the feeling that he knew exactly what she was about. But just as she began to squirm, he said, "I went to college with them. I lived in Chicago until about five years ago." As he said it, he dropped his gaze to the top of the table and Lucinda guessed that there were specific reasons he'd left Chicago. And whatever those reasons were, they weren't good things. She'd dealt with enough grief in her life to recognize sorrow when she saw it.

Her heart hurt for him. But she wasn't getting wrapped up in his problems, because doing that would mean that she still cared about him and she didn't. Not like that, anyway.

So she focused on keeping things light. "Wow—I had no idea you were here." Not that she would have done anything about it if she had. "What were you doing in Chicago? I mean, I knew you were going to go to college here, but I'd always assumed you'd gone right back to Cedar Point after you graduated and worked at the creamery."

He shrugged in that way he had. "College, at first. And then law school—"

"Wait, wait—law school?" She sat back in her chair and looked at him with new eyes. "You went to *law school*?"

"You don't have to be quite so shocked by it," he said with an easy smile.

Her cheeks heated. "No, I didn't mean— I mean, well, you were always really smart, you just…"

"Never did my homework?" His eyes crinkled as his smile deepened. "Yeah, I know. That maturity thing, it did a number on me. I grew up. I had to."

He said the last bit with that hint of sorrow again. And Lucinda knew what he was talking about.

They'd all had to grow up very fast after Gary had died.

She cleared her throat and caught sight of their waitress approaching with their drinks. "So, you're a lawyer. That's great! What's your specialty?"

Josh took a long pull on his stout. "I don't practice. My grandfather thought it would be a good idea if I knew corporate law—and I have to admit he was right—but I'm the CEO of Calhoun Creamery.

So you weren't really that far off. I went home and started in the family business. Grandpa says hi, by the way."

"Really? He remembers me?"

Josh gave her a long look that made her stomach flutter—and her pulse flutter. And her eyelashes—they fluttered, too. Suddenly, she was one giant fluttering mass, like a butterfly having a seizure or something.

"Lucy," he said, and there was no missing the fact that his voice was deeper. It set off another round of quivering and she couldn't do anything but sit there and listen to what he had to say. "You're kind of unforgettable, you know that?"

Four

"Oh," Lucy gasped, which did some very interesting things to her chest.

Not that Josh was noticing her chest at the moment. He was also not noticing the way her cheeks colored prettily—nothing like the tomato red that she'd turned yesterday. No, this was a delicate pinking of her cheeks, and something inside Josh responded on a physical level that he hadn't anticipated and sure as hell couldn't control.

He hadn't been aiming for flattery. He knew Lucy too well to think that flattery would get him anywhere. He thought he was just being honest. She *was* unforgettable. The other day he'd recognized her the second he came around the corner and clapped eyes on her.

But seeing her physical reaction?

That feeling hit him again deep in his gut—*want*. Okay, so maybe it wasn't as unexpected as it had been yesterday, when it had caught him off guard. But it was still so new and unfamiliar that he honestly didn't know what to do with it. Should he compliment her again? Tell her how much he'd missed her? Should he tell her how lonely he'd been for the last five years?

All right, so the answer was clearly *no* on that one. No. He was in no mood to come off as pitiful and needy, a widower who was lost without the touch of a woman to soothe his wounded soul, blah, blah, *blah*.

He didn't want to tell her about Sydney. And he didn't want to talk about Gary, either. Or even his parents, for that matter. He didn't want to talk about people he'd lost, because that was in the past and there was no changing it. He just wanted to keep moving forward.

Plus, he'd made a promise to Lucy. This was just dinner between two old friends. He was out of practice when it came to flirting and seduction and, given the rough ending to their friendship back in high school, he didn't really think testing the waters with her was a smart idea.

Which meant he didn't know what he was supposed to do next.

Lucy came to his rescue, though. "Do you know,"

she said, and he didn't miss the way her voice was slightly softer than it had been just a moment ago, "you're the only person who's called me Lucy in years? I mean, besides my mom."

"And your father?"

She sighed wearily but waved away the comment. "He passed from a heart attack about six years ago."

So much for getting away from the subject of people they'd lost. "I'm sorry to hear that. I didn't know."

"Thank you," she said, but she didn't sound like she was on the verge of an emotional collapse. "My mom went through a brief period where every time she saw me, she would say, 'If only you'd been a cardiologist, Lucy,' but she got over it. It's fine. She misses him—I miss him—but no one lives forever. It was his time."

Josh gaped at her. He remembered Gary's funeral. It had almost destroyed her—and then he couldn't help but feel he'd finished the job. "I guess as an oncologist, you deal with death every day?"

She nodded and took another drink. "It does go with the territory. I won't say it's gotten easier over the years, but I've come to accept that I can't save everyone." Incredibly, she even managed a small smile. "Although I do try."

Josh drained half of his bottle of beer in one swig. He hated this town. Everyone and everything in it represented an ongoing, never-ending struggle between life and death, but it seemed to him that death won a hell of a lot more than life did.

Desperately, he changed subjects. "Seems to me that you've been pretty successful at that. You're the youngest-ever head of the oncology department at Midwest—and the first woman. I could be wrong, but I'm guessing that they don't give those titles to just anyone."

Her eyes got wide again and he was struck by their light blue color, with a touch of gray around the edges. Something rare and wonderful and completely Lucy. "Did you look me up?"

"Of course," he said, figuring a little internet stalking was no big deal between friends. "I even read some of your published papers."

Her eyes narrowed and an old feeling of being busted floated up out of the past. Then she grinned at him. "You always were a terrible liar."

Josh laughed. This was better. Lucy might be unforgettable, but he had sort of forgotten how much fun it was to talk to her. She had always held his feet to the fire and expected more out of him. "Okay, okay— you got me. But I did read the titles of some of your papers, and some of them had a very helpful opening paragraph that summarized things in words I almost understood." She giggled, a sweet sound, and he heard himself say, "You're really quite brilliant, you know." Which even he knew was straight-up flirting.

There was that blush again. It made her look soft and, in a way, almost vulnerable.

Josh's arms began to itch with an unfamiliar urge to pull her against him, to settle his hands around her waist, to pull those massive glasses off her face and tilt her head back and…

What the hell was wrong with him? Seriously, aside from his sisters hugging him, he hadn't touched anyone in the last five years. But now he'd spent no more than thirty-five minutes, tops, with Lucy Wilde and suddenly he could barely control himself?

Thankfully, the waitress came back with Lucy's salad and Josh ordered another beer. He didn't normally drink quite as much as he had in the last thirty-six hours, but this was Chicago. He needed all the liquid courage he could handle.

"So tell me about you," he went on. He wasn't trying to make her blush, but the fact that it kept happening was… Well, it was something.

She gave him a look as she poured her dressing over her lettuce. "There's not much to tell. I went to college, I went to med school, I did my residencies, I do my job. It's a good job and I like doing it. We're making a lot of progress on alternative therapies and targeting the DNA structures of malignant cells and…" She wrinkled her nose in a way that Josh might have called adorable if the gesture hadn't been paired with one of Lucy's cut-the-crap looks. "I'm going to eat this salad and you're going to tell me about you because I, unlike *some* people at this table, have not Googled anyone recently." And then she shoved a huge forkful of salad into her mouth.

Josh couldn't help but grin at her. There was something comforting about the fact that, after all these years, Lucy was still just as snarky as she had ever been. "I'm sure there's more to tell than that." Her eyes narrowed at this. She chewed vigorously and held up her fork as if she were going to stab him in the hand with it. "Okay, I get the hint." Now it was his turn to feel uncomfortable because—

Because of Sydney.

"So you went to college with the Newports?" Lucy said in between bites.

"Yup. I met Graham first and then I became friends with all three of them. I was a little lost my first year." Which was kind of an understatement. He'd spent his freshman year in a daze. He'd been homesick and, because he'd lost Gary and, in a different way, Lucy, he felt very alone. "We all got along pretty well. They didn't seem to mind that I was a country bumpkin."

Lucy rolled her eyes at him. "I hate it when you do that," she said. "You were always underselling yourself back in high school. Used to drive me nuts."

He'd never really thought of it in those terms. "I wasn't underselling myself," he said defensively. "I was just immature as all hell."

She smirked at him. "No argument here."

He gave her a dull look. "If I was so immature, how come you put up with me?"

The question hung in the air and Lucy was the one to look away first. In that moment, Josh had to wonder if they would've been friends if it hadn't been for Gary. Maybe she had been right yesterday when she'd said that they couldn't be friends anymore.

"Because you're a good person," Lucy said in a quiet voice. "I mean, you were the heir to the Calhoun Creamery fortune. You could've easily been a selfish, egotistical bully of a boy. Who would've stopped you? You were cute and charming and you could have run that entire town into the ground. And you didn't."

Josh didn't know what to say to that. Yes, he'd always been destined for the creamery. But his parents—God rest their souls—and his grandparents had never handed him a single thing on a silver platter.

"I always admired you for that," Lucy added. "You were an honorable man then and, even though you might have made me a *little* mad yesterday, it's clear that's still who you are. You came to Chicago to help some friends out and brokered a peace between two groups of people who've been driving me crazy for weeks. Of course," she went on in an unnaturally perky voice, "if you barge into a medical decision like that again, I'll take back what I said about you."

"That would be terrible," he agreed just as their pizza was delivered to the table. "You have no idea how good this smells. Iowa doesn't have a clue how to make pizza."

They both scooped slices onto their plates and began to eat. The silence stretched between them, but it wasn't uncomfortable. Josh was still trying to break down what Lucy had said and reconcile it with everything that had happened in the last twenty-four hours. There was almost too much information to process.

"So," Lucy finally said in between bites of pizza, "how long did you live in Chicago?"

"Almost twelve years. I used to work for the Newports." She was gaping at him. "What?"

She shrugged. "Just having trouble reconciling the guy who used to take me cow tipping with a corporate lawyer who worked for the Newports."

Josh couldn't help but laugh at that. "It's been a long time since I tipped a cow. Don't tell my grandpa," he hurried to add.

"You really have grown up," she said. And before Josh could think of anything to say to that, her phone buzzed. "Sorry," she said, digging into her purse. "It's probably the Winchesters. Just a moment."

"No worries. Take your time." He finished his first slice of pizza and dove into a second while Lucy stared at her phone, texting and grimacing. With a heavy sigh, she dropped her phone back in her purse. "Sorry," she said again. "I'm basically always on call. Especially when it comes to certain, shall we say, *difficult* patients."

"Everything okay?"

"That was Grace—have you met her?" Josh shook his head no. He would've answered out loud, but a proper Chicago pizza had a lot of cheese and he was still chewing. "She was telling me that they've got everything set up for her father at home and she wanted to know when I can come by and check it out."

Josh finally got past the cheese and took another drink of beer. "I owe you an apology, you know."

Everything about Lucy went stiff. It almost looked as if she was expecting a brawl to break out. "Oh?"

"For yesterday. It was never my intention to undermine you or make you look bad in front of your patients. I know how dedicated you are, but—"

"But you were just doing what you always do, Josh. Keeping the peace."

That didn't exactly clarify whether or not she was in a forgiving mood. But, then again, she had come to dinner with him and she hadn't stabbed him with her fork, so that had to count for something, right? "What are you going to do? That is, if you can tell me."

"I think I can. I've got surgery in the morning and the rest of my day is packed, so it looks like I'll be going over after dinner tomorrow night to check out the room." Her shoulders slumped and he could tell that she was not happy with this development. "They're basically buying the hospital's cancer pavilion expansion, and for that I had to agree to spend nights at the Winchester estate for as long as it takes."

This was his fault. And, more than that, he felt responsible for making it better. That wouldn't be easy, balancing what Carson and his brothers wanted against what the Winchester girls wanted, all while making sure he didn't undermine Lucy's authority.

"Tell me how I can help," he said earnestly. Because there had to be a way to make this work.

Lucy gave him a measured look. "I suppose convincing everyone that Sutton's better off in the hospital is out of the question?"

He had a feeling it was, but he said, "I can give it a try."

She shook her head, but she was smiling when she did it. "I appreciate that, but we both know that ship has sailed." She wiped her mouth on her napkin and tossed it onto her plate. She'd only had one piece of pizza and her salad. Somehow, Josh had eaten most of the rest by himself.

She had promised him one dinner. But that didn't seem like it would be enough, not now. "You know," he said in a casual tone, "the thing I miss most about Chicago is the food. The pizza, the Korean barbecue, the Indian naan—we have a Chinese restaurant back in Cedar Point now, and it's not bad. But it's not like what you can get here." He steeled himself for the rejection he was pretty sure was coming, but he asked anyway. "Let me take you out to dinner tomorrow night before you go over to the Winchesters. I don't know about you, but I would kill for some Thai food."

He wasn't necessarily asking her out on a date, right? No more than he'd asked her out on a date tonight. They were old friends, so why not catch up over dinner?

But he wasn't being honest with himself. Because the difference between having dinner with Lucy and having dinner with Carson or Graham or Brooks was so huge as to be laughable. The Newport boys were his best friends, but when he looked at them he didn't get the feeling in his gut that previously he'd thought was out of his reach forever.

He and Lucy were friends. And he *had* always liked her.

She wasn't looking at him. She had placed her fingers on top of the tablecloth and was staring down at them, and he got the feeling that she was about to deliver bad news. Hell.

Then she said, "I don't think I'll have time," which was not the same thing as *no, I won't.* "I have a busy day tomorrow and then I'll have to go home and pack up so that I can move out to the Winchester estate for who knows how long. I'm sorry."

"You know," Josh said, trying to keep from laughing at her, "they have this thing now—maybe you've heard of it? It's called 'takeout.' Modern technology at its finest. You order the food and then—it's the latest thing—you take it home and eat it there."

And just like that, they were back in high school. He was teasing her and she was glaring at him, and then she picked up her napkin and threw it at his head. He dodged and they both started laughing.

It felt good to laugh again. It wasn't that he hadn't

laughed in the last five years. So maybe it just felt good to laugh with Lucy again.

When they finally quieted down—after several judgmental looks from other diners—Josh tried again. "I got you into this mess, sort of. The least I can do is bring you food and carry your luggage."

"You're right," she said with a smirk that meant that he had it coming and he had no choice but to sit there and let her cut him to shreds. "It is the least you can do. You're on. I like pad see ew—medium hot plus." She dug around in her purse until she came up with the stub of a pencil and a scrap of paper. She wrote down her address and slid it over the table to him. "I should get home by six thirty and, I told Grace Winchester that I would try to be out to the estate by eight thirty. That doesn't give us a lot of time."

That made Josh's eyebrows jump up. *Time for what?* He had meant it when he said this was just dinner—but was something else on the menu?

"To eat and get packed," Lucy hurried to add, her eyes getting wide again.

He couldn't fight the grin that took hold of his lips. Sure, this was still just friends having dinner. But there was no mistaking it—she had thought the same thing he had.

"I'm looking forward to it."

Whatever *it* wound up being, he was looking very forward to it.

Five

Despite the fact that Lucinda had told Josh that she would get home about six thirty, she managed to get home at six. True, she had to bend the truth to get out of the meeting with John Jackson by saying, "I've got to run—the Winchesters, you know."

It wasn't entirely a lie. She was heading over to the Winchester estate that very evening to set up camp.

But first she found herself doing some last-minute cleaning while simultaneously trying to apply mascara without putting out her own eye.

Needless to say, it was not going well. She'd gone—what? Six months without wearing mascara? Yes, the last time she'd caked it on had been to go to that gala fund-raiser for the hospital. Coinciden-tally, that was also the last time she'd worn her dress.

Yet here she was wearing mascara for the second time in two days. And why?

Josh Calhoun. A man she'd convinced herself she never wanted to see ever again.

Six thirty came and went. Then six thirty-one. Six thirty-two.

Oh, God, she was going to drive herself insane. She forced herself to stand in front of her meager closet. What exactly did one wear when sleeping over at the billionaire's estate to make sure that he got his cancer treatments on time? Somehow, her fleecy pa-jama bottoms featuring frolicking penguins didn't seem quite right.

In general, frolicking penguins did not exactly scream professionalism and medical authority.

Maybe she would just sleep in a pair of her dress slacks. She'd be rumpled, but at least she wouldn't be humiliated.

Her buzzer sounded, making her jump. Six thirty-six. That could still be reasonably construed as being on time.

She hurried to the intercom. "Yes?"

"I have pad thai," Josh promised over the stat-icky intercom.

She pushed the button that would let him in. "Come on up." Although she didn't know how she was going to eat at this moment.

Her stomach was a hot mess, and as much as she

tried to tell herself it was simply because she was about to put herself at the mercy of the Winchesters and the Newports for an indeterminate amount of time, that wasn't it. That wasn't it by a long shot.

No, the reason she was nervous was knocking on her door. "Lucy?"

She took a deep breath and opened the door. She hadn't thought of herself as Lucy in so long that the name still sounded weird. But she couldn't imagine Josh calling her anything else.

He was leaning against her door frame, his arms full of grocery bags. "Good Lord!" she gasped as she stared at the bags.

"Dinner is served," he said in what could only be described as a gallant voice. He stepped into her apartment and then, before she could process what he was doing, he leaned down and kissed her on the forehead. "I have Thai," he said, leaning back but not stepping clear. "A bottle of California Chardonnay and some ice cream from this new place I've heard of—Calhoun Creamery?" He winked at her. "I hope it's good. I got you mint chocolate chip."

Lucinda knew that she needed to do something or say something. Maybe even shut the door. But he had just short-circuited her brain.

He'd kissed her. He'd remembered what her favorite kind of ice cream was.

And more than any of that, he was *here*.

Josh was still standing over her, smiling down as

if he was enjoying her complete and total befuddlement. "I'll just put this in the kitchen, shall I?"

"Oh. Yes." She gestured in the general direction of her kitchen and managed to get her door shut. She was suddenly very aware of why, exactly, having Josh at her place made her so twitchy.

It was because they were alone. Dinner at the pizzeria last night had been out in public. But right now?

It was him and her. And some Thai food.

She realized that she had never had a man over to her apartment before. Which sounded pathetic, but it was the truth. At almost the exact same instant, she remembered the last time she'd been alone with Josh—that awful night she'd embarrassed herself so completely in front of him.

Right. He may have kissed her, but a friendly little peck on the forehead wasn't any kind of seduction. Therefore, it wouldn't do for her to act like this was anything more than a continuation of their conversation last night. They were friends. And there was no way she was going to risk humiliation a second time.

Josh Calhoun was off-limits.

She surveyed what seemed like enough food for a dinner party for ten. "Josh, how much food did you buy?"

"This?" Josh looked at the chaos he had unleashed on her kitchen island. "It's just some pad see ew, pad thai, crab rangoon, egg rolls, rice—it's not that much."

"You know it's just the two of us, right?"

He paused in the process of putting the ice cream in the freezer. "Actually, I wasn't one hundred percent sure. It's possible you have a roommate or... someone." He shut the freezer with more force than was necessary. Then he turned and gave her that easy grin. "We didn't discuss that at dinner the other night."

She blinked at him. "I'm not seeing anyone." Which was the truth. However, it also neatly sidestepped the fact that she had never really seen anyone except for Gary. But she was doing her best to avoid sounding pathetic on what was still probably not a real date, so she left that part out. "You?"

"No." Considering that he was the one who had brought up significant others, his clipped tone seemed out of character. "Let me get the wine open. Can you get some glasses?"

Oh. Right. She stepped around him—her kitchen was small—and got two matching glasses out of the cabinet. They weren't wineglasses, but at least they were clean. She gave them to Josh and then got out the plates and the silverware.

"Nice place," Josh said as he poured them each a glass of wine. "Have you lived here long?"

"About four years—since I joined Midwest."

"You have a hell of a view," he said, looking out toward the living room with its floor-to-ceiling windows.

She'd arranged the couch so that it faced the windows instead of the flat-screen television she only used to watch movies. She didn't have drapes or anything on those windows. She hadn't wanted anything between her and the sky and the water.

She glanced at him out of the corner of her eye. "To be honest, most of the time I eat on the couch so that I can watch the colors at sunset."

"Then by all means," Josh said, grabbing a plate and loading it up.

They carried their plates and wine over to the couch and settled in. The sun was just beginning to set behind the building, and the sky over Lake Michigan was going from blue to pink and orange. They ate for few moments before Lucinda worked up the nerve to ask him about that clipped *no*. "I'm surprised."

"About what?" Josh asked around a mouthful of crab rangoon.

"That you're not seeing anyone. I always assumed you'd settle down, have some kids." She knew immediately that it was the wrong thing to have said. She would have given anything to be able to take it back. But it was too late. The question hung over Josh like a dark cloud, and not even the brilliant sunset already fading into purple could burn it away.

"I'm sorry," she said quickly. God, she was an idiot. Because his reaction could only mean one thing.

He had done just that and it hadn't worked out.

"Don't be." His tone was casual, but she heard how forced it was. "It was just one of those things."

She wasn't buying that for a second. "Do you want to talk about it?"

"Not really. But I don't want to hide things from you." He set his plate on the coffee table and leaned back, his eyes fixed at some point way out over the lake. "Sydney. Her name was Sydney."

Was. That was possibly the worst word in the English language. *Was.*

"Graham Newport introduced us in my junior year. And, man, I was gone from the start."

She needed to say something here, something comforting and understanding that still kept things light. She was, after all, a professional at this sort of conversation. She had them weekly—daily, even. Bad news and loss were her constant companions.

But Josh wasn't her patient and Lucinda simply didn't know what to say.

He slid a sideways glance at her. "She was smart and fierce and she made me toe the line." He grinned, but it was a sad thing. It made Lucy's chest hurt. "She made me laugh. She's the reason I made it through law school. She didn't like it when I undersold myself, either. You would've loved her, Lucy."

"I would have," Lucy murmured. "You needed that."

"Yeah."

Silence fell between them as darkness fell outside.

Too late, Lucy realized that she didn't have any lights on in the apartment. One moment, she and Josh were sitting in a nearly light room. The next, they were in almost total darkness. "You asked why I left Chicago," Josh said in the darkness. "My life here was with her. And when she died…"

Lucy nodded, belatedly realizing that he probably couldn't see her. There was something comforting about the darkness, where she couldn't see his expression and he couldn't see hers. "So you went back to Cedar Point."

"I did."

They were quiet for some time longer. Lucy finished her wine and sat forward, leaving her glass on the coffee table next to the remains of her dinner.

When she sat back, her shoulder brushed against Josh's. It was another innocent touch, much like his kiss on her forehead earlier. But at the same time, it wasn't.

Josh shifted and his arm came around her shoulders. She wasn't sure if he pulled her against him or she was the one who moved first. The outcome was the same either way. She curled up against the side, her arm around his waist and her head against his shoulder as he held her.

There was an intimacy to the moment, but for once Lucy didn't overthink it. Josh had been right—they would always be friends. Right now, she wanted to let her friend know she was here for him and that she understood. More than anyone, she understood.

She didn't know how much time passed before Josh spoke again. "I didn't really mean for that to be quite such a downer." His voice was low and soft in her ear.

"It's okay." And, honestly, it was. "In case you've forgotten, I'm an oncologist. Death is a part of my life. You don't have to apologize for it."

He squeezed her tight. "Thank you," he said in a voice so quiet she had to look up to make sure she'd heard him correctly.

"For what?"

Somehow, she knew that he was looking down at her even though the room was almost pitch-black. Then he shifted and his fingertips brushed against her cheek and traced a path along her jaw. "For not telling me to get over it or move on or that it was God's will. Because that's what people always say and I hate it."

His fingers continued to move over her cheek in a slow, stroking motion. She wasn't surprised at what he'd said—she'd heard it all and more. "I would never dismiss your grief like that," she told him. Objectively, she knew all about the stages of grief and how people processed their loss.

But she wasn't thinking objectively right now. The arm that was around her side moved and his hand slid over her ribs and down her waist. She knew without even having to see that he was getting closer to her. She could feel the heat radiating off his chest, and the warmth of his breath against her forehead and then her nose. When he spoke again, she could feel the ghost of his lips moving against hers. "I missed you, Lucy."

This was wrong. So, *so* wrong. He was still in love with his wife and Lucy was married to her job, and it seemed as if there was something she was supposed to be doing right now—something that did not involve melting against him and trying to decide if she would wait for his kiss or just take one herself.

But she couldn't think of anything except Josh. Her hand skimmed up his chest and over his jaw and then there was no more space between them.

Once, she'd kissed him. She didn't remember very much of it because she'd been upset and desperate, and then there'd been the dawning horror that not only was he not kissing her back, but he was pushing her away and saying he couldn't do "this."

The memory was so painful that, for a moment, she was physically locked up with panic. She couldn't handle the humiliation, not again.

And then Josh sighed into her mouth, a sound of satisfaction and need like she'd never heard before, and Lucy stopped thinking about that first, terrible kiss. Instead, she lost herself in his lips and his arms. Here, in the dark, it was okay. Everything was okay and getting better by the second.

Then his tongue traced the seam of her lips and she opened for him and everything went from being okay to something else—something entirely different. Better. Hotter.

Because, all of a sudden, Lucy's skin started to

tingle and her heart pounded and, unexpectedly, her nipples tightened to the point of pain—so much so that she arched her back to get closer to Josh in an effort to relieve the pressure. His sigh turned into a growl, a noise that she felt throughout her entire body. The space between her legs grew hot and heavy and the pressure was maddening.

It scared her a little, the intensity of the physiological responses that blossomed out of nowhere. Because suddenly, after years of convincing herself she did not need a physical relationship with a man—that she didn't need any physical relationship at all—she realized what a lie that had been.

She needed this. She needed *him*.

And she needed him now. She shifted, unsure of how to ask for what she wanted—unsure of what it was exactly that she wanted. But the pressure on her nipples and the weight between her legs were pushing her toward *something*.

As she tried to adjust her angle toward Josh, he surprised her by lifting her onto his lap. She straddled him, which made everything better and worse at the same time. "God, Lucy," he groaned before his hands slid down her back and his mouth captured hers again.

He gripped her bottom and settled her against him more firmly. She whimpered as his erection made contact with her, hard and hot between her legs. All she could think was, *finally*. After all these years, she was *finally* going to find out what everyone else in the whole wide world already knew about.

Her head fell back as Josh ground against her, but he kept kissing her. His lips trailed down her neck and she arched into him again, her body begging for things she didn't have the words for. She was bracketed in his arms as his mouth moved lower. He grabbed the placket of her shirt in his teeth and pulled it to the side, exposing the top of her breast.

"I want this," she managed to say as she loosened her grip on him long enough to undo the stubborn buttons. This must be why people were always ripping shirts off in movies—buttons took too damn long.

Finally, she got three of the stupid things open. That was as far as she got before Josh was pushing her up and his mouth closed over her breast. Even though Lucy still had her bra on, the feeling of his mouth on her body was electric. Synapses and neurons all fired at once and the result had her shivering and shaking in his arms.

She wished she could see him. That was the only thing she'd change about this moment.

"Let me, babe," Josh said against her skin as she clung to him. His hands moved—one had stayed on her bottom and the other came around the front to cup her breast. He pulled her bra aside and then his lips wrapped around her nipple and his teeth were on her skin and—and—and—

"Josh!" His name was on her lips and his mouth

was on her body, and she wanted this like she'd never wanted anything else. She'd always wanted this.

"That's it, Lucy. I just want to…" His voice trailed off as he reached between her legs and began to stroke over the seam of her pants.

Lucy moaned. She understood the biology of the human female body. But she knew *nothing*. Nothing compared with what Josh was effortlessly doing to her. He sucked at her breast, gripped her bottom and rubbed her clit and there wasn't a single thing Lucinda could do about any of it. She was helpless in his arms and if she was making a fool of herself, then so be it.

She bore down on his hand and buried her fingers in his hair as she held him against her breast. Just when she didn't think she could take it for another second, Josh groaned, "Lucy," and she lost whatever control over herself she'd been clinging to.

She climaxed in his arms with such force that she almost pitched herself right off his lap. "Oh, God," she whispered in a shaky voice as Josh gathered her back in his arms and pulled her against his chest.

"You're beautiful," he got out before he was kissing her again with even more urgency.

She wasn't sure she could buy that—she wasn't beautiful and, besides, it was pitch-black in this room. But he grabbed her bottom again and was grinding up against her, and even though she didn't think she could handle another climax like that, she could already feel the pressure building again.

"You," she tried to tell him in an authoritative voice. "Your turn."

His only response was to groan as she shifted against him. She didn't know what she was doing, but that didn't seem to matter. She kissed him and let her body move as it wanted to and—

Her phone buzzed and lit up, an unwelcome spotlight in their dark little world. Lucy jolted against him. "Ignore that," she told him. Whoever it was, they could just call back later. There was nothing in the world so important as what was happening right now between her and Josh.

Then he had to ruin it by asking, "What time is it?"

She froze. There was something that she was maybe supposed to be doing right now—she was supposed to be at the Winchester estate, seeing if they'd gotten a room set up for Sutton Winchester so he could continue his treatment at home.

"Oh, crap—the Winchesters." She pulled away from Josh and threw herself off the couch. She managed to get a light turned on without breaking anything and hurried to her phone. Yep, it was a series of texts from Nora Winchester, asking her where she was and if she was still planning on stopping by. "Oh, crap," she repeated again. It was nine o'clock.

She was late. God, how she hated being late. People depended on her. The least she could do was be dependable. Instead, she'd been throwing herself at Josh Calhoun—the very last person she should be screwing around with. She'd completely lost her mind, hadn't she? Because she was not the kind of person who put something as fleeting as physical desire ahead of her duties and responsibilities. There were lives on the line, damn it. She knew that.

But Josh had made her forget for a few glorious, humiliating moments. He'd made her forget everything, including herself. Especially herself. Shame burned at her cheeks and she couldn't meet his gaze when he said, "Lucy?"

One simple rule—she was not to embarrass herself in front of Josh. Not again. Never again.

And she'd done just that.

Damn it all.

Six

Josh sat on the couch in a state of shock. What the hell had just happened?

One minute, he was enjoying good Thai food with an old friend, watching the sunset over Lake Michigan and not actively hating Chicago.

The next, they were wrapped up in each other, hands and mouths everywhere. Although Josh was a little out of practice, he was pretty sure he'd made it good for her. He wasn't some green boy anymore. Lucy had moaned and writhed and shuddered against him, and damned if it hadn't been good. Amazing, even.

And then, just like all the light switches Lucy was actively flipping on, the whole thing was over and done.

He scrubbed his hand over his face and willed his erection to stand way the hell down as he tried to make sense of the situation. He wasn't having a lot of luck at that. He hadn't wanted—really and truly *wanted*—in such a damned long time that the whole thing had turned his brain into mush.

He shifted, trying to figure out what he needed to do next.

"I can't…" Lucy muttered. "I don't even know what to pack. And I'm late!"

That's what she was thinking about? He was trying to figure out how he could finish what they'd started together and she was worried about being *late*? "Lucy."

Not that she listened. She didn't. "I can't be late, Josh. I'm never late."

Well. At least she was acknowledging he was still in the room. "Why do you have to pack?"

"Because I'm supposed to stay at the house while Sutton's being treated," she replied, looking at him as if he were a special kind of stupid.

That made no sense. "But I thought he was still in the hospital?"

"He is," she snapped and then he thought she muttered something about…penguins?

He shook his head again, trying to get the blood to start flowing to his brain instead of other parts. He could still feel Lucy's weight as she straddled him, so close… "You're not going to discharge him tonight, are you?"

"Of course not!"

"Why are you packing right now, then?"

Lucy came to a dead stop. "What?" she asked in utter confusion.

Josh forced himself to stand, although this was not much more comfortable than sitting had been. "If Sutton isn't going home tonight, why do you need to stay there tonight?"

"I…don't?" She was completely, if adorably, flustered. "I guess I thought I should—I don't know—already have my stuff over there? Before he got there?"

Josh couldn't help but grin at her. One of the smartest people he'd ever known—and she hadn't made that mental leap. "You know, there's such a thing as being too prepared."

She shot him one hell of a mean look—easily the meanest look she'd given him since he'd first seen her again. But if she was trying to scare him off, it wasn't working. In fact, it was having the opposite effect.

Because all he wanted to do was walk over there and kiss her until she stopped scowling at him.

He didn't, though. Being married for seven years had taught him a few things and he wasn't so slow as to forget what those things were. Kissing her right now would guarantee failure.

So, instead, he grabbed his keys and said, "Come on, let's go."

"What?"

"Let's go."

"You're not coming with me," she said in a tone of voice that made it clear this point was not up for discussion.

Except it was. "Yes, I am. Come on." He opened her door. And then he waited because he knew damn well she wasn't going to fall in line that easily. Not his Lucy.

Then he caught himself. When had she become his Lucy?

The moment he'd kissed her.

"No, you're *not*." It was at that point that Josh realized she might actually punch him. At the very least, she wanted to.

Unexpectedly, a wave of guilt hit him. "You've had some wine and you're upset." He hadn't thought it possible, but her glare got even meaner. This was going from bad to worse. "And we need to talk."

"No, we don't. Nothing to talk about." She grabbed her purse, slung it over her shoulder and began to wrangle her hair back into some semblance of order. "And you've had some wine, too."

He grinned at her again, not that she saw. He easily had sixty, maybe seventy pounds on her and he'd had half a glass of wine. "Lucy."

She stopped her frenetic movements, but she didn't meet his eyes. She didn't say anything, either. He had that odd sensation of guilt again—that he'd embarrassed her.

True, he'd kissed her—but she'd kissed him back. Enthusiastically. And he was pretty sure that she had said, "I want this," and he was even surer that she'd told him it was his turn.

So why the hell was she so embarrassed?

He tried a different approach. "I want to drive you. I want to spend more time with you."

She took a step back and he saw that she hadn't been ready for that line of attack. "You can't," she said definitively. "Patient privacy."

He had to go with his ace in the hole. She was not going to be happy about this. "Carson asked me to stop by the Winchester estate and make sure that everything was in order." Which was not something Josh was happy about. But he'd mentioned he was going to have dinner with Lucy before she went out to the Winchester estate and Carson had made his request. Josh had almost forgotten about it while he'd been in Lucy's arms and it about killed him to bring it up now.

The color drained out of Lucy's face.

"Oh. I see." And just like that, she shut down. It hurt to watch. "Well. If you've been invited by family, then by all means."

She stalked past him, her head held high and her eyes focused anywhere but where he stood. He knew, without a doubt, that he was screwed.

As he followed her down the stairs, he tried to think—what would Sydney say? They'd had their share of disagreements and occasional fights in the ten years that they'd known each other. And Josh was known for being a peacemaker. He was the one who smoothed over fights, not the one who made them worse.

Which was clearly what he had done right now.

Lucy was not Sydney. While the two women probably would've gotten along and maybe even been friends, they were not the same woman. Appearances had been very important to Sydney. When a woman started her own high-end interior design business, appearances were everything. For her, Josh had willingly put away his hats and shoved his shit-kicker boots into the back of the closet. He'd worn corporate suits with the lawyerly ties because having a professional husband who made her look good had made Sydney happy.

Lucy, on the other hand… Today she wore basically the same outfit she'd been wearing at the hospital work site. A blouse, some dark slacks and her lab coat. She didn't have coordinating jewelry and her hair had a mind of its own. At best, her shoes could be described as serviceable—the round-toe things with thick heels that so many medical professionals wore.

She hadn't really changed that much. Exchange the slacks for jeans and the blouses for sweatshirts and she looked almost exactly the same as she had in high school.

Except for the curves. The soft, luscious curves that he had had in his hands for way too short a period of time. The Lucy he remembered had been someone who hadn't blossomed yet. Maybe that was why she had always fit in with him and Gary so well—she'd been something of a tomboy and had certainly looked the part. No one in their right mind would have ever accused Sydney of being a tomboy.

No one in their right mind would have ever asked Sydney Laurence to go cow tipping on a Saturday night. But Lucy used to.

They made it out of the building and Josh pointed toward where he'd parked his truck. Lucy froze again. "Wait—you're still driving that truck?"

"Yeah. Is that a problem?"

"No…" He glanced down at her and saw that she was worrying her bottom lip—the very same lip he himself had been worrying not twenty minutes ago. "I would've figured you'd had a new car since then. That thing has to be twenty, twenty-five years old."

"Close. It's nineteen years old. I had the engine completely rebuilt about five years ago." When he'd come home from Chicago, actually. But he didn't tell her that part. "It looks like hell, but it runs great." He held the door for her.

She still had her car keys in her hand. "Do you even know where you're going? This isn't Cedar Point, you know. This is Chicago."

"Believe it or not, I know my way around this town. And after my last conversation with Carson, I programmed the Winchester estate address into my directions."

Lucy sighed and climbed up into the truck. As gallantly as he could, Josh closed the door—which took a bit of force, since he didn't use the passenger side door much and parts of it had rusted. Then he went around to the driver's side, climbed in and started the truck. The engine gurgled and then roared to life as he called up the directions on his phone.

They drove in silence for a few minutes. For once, traffic was not horrendous as they headed up the North Shore toward the Winchester estate.

Josh was at a loss as to what he was supposed to say now. If it were anyone else but Lucy sitting in the car next to him—anyone but a woman he had been kissing and hoping to do a whole lot more with—he would've known what to say. What was it about her that tied him in knots?

Wait, don't answer that, he told himself.

So he said nothing while the silence between them grew heavy. He didn't regret kissing her, though. He didn't regret touching her, either. He wanted to do it again. For the first time in five years, he wanted to hold a woman in his arms and lose himself in her touch and her sounds and her body.

Maybe that was part of the problem. He hadn't done this dance in such a long time—long before Sydney had died. He was thirty-five and the last time he'd started a new relationship had been fifteen years ago. He was rusty and it was showing.

But he wanted Lucy. It didn't make complete sense to him, but he *wanted* her. He wanted to go back to being tangled up with her on the couch in the dark and listening to her sigh his name. He wanted to know he could still do that for a woman.

He wanted to feel alive again, and for a few short minutes that was how Lucy had made him feel. No one else had given that to him.

And if he didn't get his head out of his ass, those few short minutes were all he was going to get.

At a stoplight, he glanced over at her. Her back was ramrod straight and her eyes were focused straight ahead. She looked almost as if he were driving her to her doom. Was that because they were going to the Winchester estate or because she was in the car with him?

Discretion was the better part of valor. "I'm sorry."

She made an indelicate snorting noise. "Is that a general all-purpose apology? Because if you're hoping that will solve the world's ills, I'm here to tell you it won't."

Damn. Not that Sydney had ever bought that lame attempt, either. So he tried again—and this time, he was very specific. "I thought you were enjoying our time on the couch. I would never do anything to hurt you. Including putting you in an awkward position."

She snorted again, this time louder. Because, yeah, even he had to admit that the inside of this truck was awkward. "I don't want to talk about it."

Crap. He was in serious trouble here and he knew it. "It won't happen again."

He hit another stoplight and glanced at her again. He wouldn't have thought it was possible, but she was sitting up even straighter now. "No. Of course not." Her voice had gotten quiet and something in her tone pulled at him.

It was that guilt again, damn it. Not the same kind of guilt he'd felt when Sydney had died.

If it was possible for guilt to feel familiar, though, this did. It niggled at the back of his mind, like an old bug bite that he'd accidentally brushed so that it suddenly itched again. "Okay, I just apologized for the wrong thing. Are you going to explain why you're mad at me or should I just keep guessing?"

She didn't even snort this time. "The light is green." The moment she said it, horns began to blare behind them.

God, he hated Chicago. Josh accelerated through the intersection and started to drive like he meant it. He hadn't expected to suddenly find himself weaving across traffic lanes like any native Chicagoan would do, but he was upset at Lucy and he was upset at himself. This whole situation stunk and he didn't know what else to do.

And he *always* knew what to do. That's what made him so good at his job. He ran the Calhoun Creamery because he had the vision to know what needed to be done to move the company into the future. He had the skills to negotiate with federal regulators and lobbyists and other dairy farmers. He had enough detachment that he could do things like walk into the middle of a fight between Eve Winchester and Carson Newport and identify the best course of action for everyone involved.

Everyone except for Lucy. He didn't have any detachment when it came to her.

It was going to be a problem. Hell, it was already a problem.

When she spoke, her voice was so soft that he almost missed it. "Do the Winchesters know you're coming? Or was your entire goal this evening to make it look like I invited you along?"

Oh. "You think I would use you like that?"

"Sutton Winchester is worth at least a billion dollars. Lots of people would do lots of things to get a piece of that. Including the Newports." She threw that out there as if that could explain everything.

Well, it didn't. "You realize I'm a multimillionaire in my own right, don't you? The Newport boys can't bribe me into doing things like that. I don't need the money and even if I did, I would *never* use you like that."

"What happened on the couch was merely…a fringe benefit, then?"

Josh was getting madder by the second. "You are acting like—"

"Oh, this I have to hear." She turned her full body toward him and stared. "How am I acting? Let me guess. Like a prim prude? Like an ice-cold bitch? Wait. I know. I'm not good enough for you. I have never been good enough for you." She paused, leaving a silence so sharp it could have cut glass. "Let me know when I'm getting close."

"No, goddamn it. Lucy, would you just listen? That's not it at all."

She crossed her arms just as Josh took a corner a little harder than he meant to. They were leaving the bright lights of Chicago proper behind. There was more open space as they moved into a more exclusive neighborhood. He was almost out of time and he was doing a piss-poor job of explaining himself. "I am not better than you. I never have been. If anything, I'm not good enough for you."

She threw her hands up. "Sure. I've heard that before, too."

"What the hell are you talking about?" Because it didn't sound like she was still talking about what happened on the couch. Enough of this crap. "You listen to me, Lucy Wilde. I like you. I have always liked you. I am *not* sorry for kissing you. I *am* sorry that we got interrupted because all I want to do is turn this truck around and take you back to your apartment and lay you out on that bed until you're screaming my name in pleasure. And the fact that I want that confuses me just as much as it confuses you because I didn't think I could still feel that anymore. So stop acting like I'm torturing you. We're not kids anymore and this is not a game I want to play. Now tell me why you're upset with me or get over it."

She didn't say anything. Again. And he honestly

didn't know if he wanted to throttle her or pull her into a hug because he was pretty sure that she was over there doing her best not to cry.

But just then they found themselves at the gate of the Winchester estate. He got buzzed in and they drove toward the house.

A valet—an actual valet at a private home—opened Lucy's door and handed her out, took Josh's keys and stared at the stick shift in his truck in confusion before Josh told him to leave it there.

Then and only then, when he and Lucy had started up the grand staircase toward the front door, did he hear Lucy's reply. "There are some things," she said without looking at him, "that you just don't 'get over.' But I don't have to tell you that, do I?"

And then, without waiting for a response, she walked into the Winchester home and left him standing on the stoop.

Seven

This was why Lucy didn't have relationships. People in general and men in specific were distracting. As Lucy looked over the proper hospital-quality room that the Winchester girls had miraculously assembled in just over twenty-four hours, she was horrified to realize that she was having trouble concentrating on the pumps and computers.

Because she was thinking of Josh.

No, that wasn't it. Not entirely. Because she was thinking of how very badly she had embarrassed herself again. When would she learn? She could not trust herself around Josh Calhoun.

At least this time, she tried to tell herself, she had not done it all by herself. Not like the last time, anyway. She had not thrown herself at Josh Calhoun and begged for him to take her. He had not pushed her away and said no. It hadn't been like that at all.

It had been soft and sweet and natural and right. The most right thing in the world.

And then it stopped. All the good feelings, all the warmth and tenderness—gone.

And she still didn't know if it was real or not. Because if he had brought dinner over to her place, given her a glass of wine and kissed her senseless for the sole purpose of guaranteeing that she would take him with her to the Winchester home, then she would never forgive him. Never. It didn't matter how many times he claimed he would never use her like that.

"Well, what do you think?" Nora Winchester said, as they stood in the room the sisters had prepared for their father.

Tonight Lucy was dealing with the third Winchester sister, Nora—and Nora's little boy, Declan. He was snuggled in his mom's arms, his head resting on her shoulder. He had one thumb stuck in his mouth and was watching Lucy with the kind of naked curiosity that only small children could successfully pull off.

Lucy felt bad because she knew that she was keeping him up. If she had gotten here when she was supposed to, Nora would already be putting her son to bed, reading him stories and tucking him in with a kiss on his forehead.

"I'm impressed," Lucy told Nora. "I didn't think you'd be able to get everything I requested."

Nora shrugged, which jostled her son. "Sometimes, there are advantages to being a Winchester."

Before Lucy could respond to that, Declan began to fidget. He twisted out of his mother's grasp and made a break for the brand-new hospital bed. Oh. That's what had his attention—Lucy had tested the buttons to raise and lower the bed, and that was too much a temptation for any one kid.

"Whoa," Josh said, neatly stepping up and swinging Declan into his arms. "Where you going, cowboy?"

Declan pointed shyly at the bed.

"I don't remember hearing you ask your mother if you could jump on the bed—or Dr. Lucy. You've always got to ask, you know that, buddy? Your grandpa is going to be in this bed and you can't just jump on him, either."

Declan looked disappointed. Then Josh said, "Why don't we ask now? Just this one time, though. When Grandpa's in the bed, we can't play on it, okay?"

Nora smiled a tired smile. "No jumping on the bed," she said in a tone of voice that made Lucy think of an old nursery rhyme. "We don't want to bump our heads. But maybe Mr. Calhoun can help you work the buttons for two minutes."

Lucy honestly didn't know who was happier about this announcement—Josh or the child. Both of their faces lit up in wide grins. "Let's go!" Josh said, carrying Declan over to the bed. They sat down together and figured out which button did what. "Whee!" they both called out.

And Lucy didn't know what to say. There was something about the way Josh played with the child that hurt her at the same time that it made her happy. Because it was a piece to a puzzle that she hadn't realized was missing.

Josh had been married. Josh had been happy.

And Josh's wife had died.

She hadn't lied earlier when she told him she'd thought he had settled down and had a couple of kids by now. Josh was the kind of man who needed kids.

"He's really quite good," Nora said.

Lucy hadn't realized that the other woman had stepped in closer. "I'm sorry?"

"With Declan. Some men look at kids as if they were feral animals with contagious diseases. You can always tell which ones are the ones who will be good fathers and which ones won't."

"How can you tell?" Lucy asked as another "whee" came from the bed. It felt like a silly question, though, because it was obvious to anyone with two eyes that Josh was having just as much fun as Declan was.

Nora gave her a look that bordered on pitying. "I want to apologize on behalf of my sisters and Carson," she said without answering the question. "I don't think it's fair that you're being asked to relocate just so you can take care of our father."

Well, that was unexpected. Lucy wasn't sure how she was supposed to respond to that. Of all the Winchester daughters, Nora was the one with whom she'd had the least interaction. Thus far, her impression of Nora Winchester was that she would rather be anywhere but here. And that was a feeling Lucy could sympathize with.

"Cancer isn't fair," she said. And she meant it. "We're doing what we can to prolong his life, but you understand that this isn't about me? With your father's kind of cancer and how it progressed in his system before he sought treatment, we're risking all our gains by moving him out of the hospital."

Nora sighed heavily. "Oh, I understand. I also understand my sisters when they say they're concerned about his privacy." She gave Lucy a sympathetic smile. "There's just no good solution and sometimes we have to do the best with what we've got. Now," she went on in a more businesslike tone, "would you like to see the guest quarters? I was told you would be bringing your bags…"

"Again, my apologies for running late. I got held up at the hospital and didn't have time to pack." It wasn't a malicious lie. She just strategically left out the fact that it had been Josh who'd been holding her up. Physically. "I'm sorry if we screwed up bedtime." She angled her body so that Josh couldn't hear what she was about to say next. "I understand that Carson has asked Mr. Calhoun to check in on things, but you are under no obligation to open your home or your father's medical treatment to him."

That got her a funny look from Nora. "Dr. Wilde—after he got Carson and Eve to agree on something? I'm thinking of inviting him to Thanksgiving!" She laughed and Lucy tried to smile. She didn't think she made it, though, because Nora went on, "Carson told me Mr. Calhoun would be by, and that you and Mr. Calhoun were friends—old friends."

So Nora had been expecting Josh? Why hadn't anyone else thought it prudent to tell her what the damned plan was?

Still, Nora's response—and complete lack of concern about Josh—reassured Lucy somewhat. "We are. But he's not a member of the family and he's not a colleague of mine. And if you're truly concerned about your father's privacy..."

Another "whee" came from the bed. Nora looked to her son. "All right, sweetie—that's enough. Why don't we show Dr. Lucy where she's going to be staying, and then it's time for you to get a story and go to bed."

Declan said, "Aw."

But Josh said, "You heard her, buddy." He scooped Declan off the bed and jostled him in his arms.

Their little party, such as it was, followed Nora out into the hall and one door down. "We thought it best to keep you close to his room," Nora said in an apologetic tone as she opened the door. "I hope that's all right."

"That's fine," Lucy said as Nora flipped on the light. And then she gawked at the guest room.

Because the guest room was almost as large as her apartment. It had a massive queen-size four-poster bed in the middle of the room done in lush shades of blue and teal, with accents of orange in the pillows and drapes. There was a sitting area with the couch and two armchairs facing a fireplace with a flat-screen TV above the mantel. Off to one side was a small wet bar, complete with a minifridge.

"Nice place," Josh said.

Nora looked at Lucy and said, "Will this do?" She pointed to the small screen that was on the table next to the bed. "We had monitors installed so you'll have visual contact at all times. And here," she said, pointing to the computer on the coffee table, "is the monitor you requested. We'll have any meals you'd like delivered to the room—we don't expect you to join us in the dining room, unless you'd like to. If there's anything else you'd like to have, just let me know."

"This should be fine," Lucy said faintly.

It wasn't fine. This whole thing was insane. When she had become the head of the oncology department at Midwest, it had not come with a stipulation in the contract that she might occasionally have to go live with her patients. She didn't want to do this.

Then she thought of the expanded cancer pavilion that the Winchesters and the Newports were going to fund and how many people that was going to help and she sucked it up.

"Assuming his numbers are where I want them to be, I should be able to discharge him tomorrow afternoon—the next day at the latest." She was trying her damnedest to sound professional at ten fifteen in the evening while watching Josh cuddle a two-year-old with such longing that it hurt. She wasn't sure she was making it. "I arranged for several of my most trusted nurses to pick up extra shifts when I cannot be on-site. As I've reminded your sisters, I will not compromise anyone else's care during this…experiment."

Nora nodded and reached out her arms for her son. Josh handed over the sleepy boy, and the look on his face…

"Can you find your way out?" Nora asked. She hugged her son and rubbed his back.

"Sure." Lucy felt almost dizzy with the surge of emotions that she couldn't name. On some level, she was still mad at Josh. And she still wanted him— which only made her madder. She didn't want to see the look of longing on Josh's face as they watched Nora carry her child to bed and she didn't want to think about what his marriage to his wife had been like. She didn't want to stay at the Winchester estate and, truthfully, she didn't want to be Sutton Winchester's oncologist anymore. But she also didn't want to turn down the chance to have that cancer pavilion bought and paid for.

As Nora had said, sometimes there were no good solutions. Lucy wished she wasn't the one who had to make the best of it. But giving a few weeks of her time to the Winchesters was for the greater good. She couldn't back out now.

Josh rested his hand on the small of her back and startled her. "Lucy?" She heard so many questions in that one word.

If only she had some answers. "I need to go home," she told him. Had he really brought her dinner and kissed her just to get out here to the estate? Or had it been a series of unfortunate coincidences? Everyone else seemed to know and accept that Josh would be here this evening.

Had he used her? Or did he really want her?

His hand was still on her lower back, warm and solid and somehow an answer to the question that she hadn't asked. "Would you like to go now?"

Her head was a mess and she didn't know what she was supposed to think anymore. "Yes," she said, turning into him. "I think I would."

Eight

The drive back to Lucy's apartment was quiet. She was probably still mad at him and he couldn't blame her for that. He'd handled the situation poorly—no doubt about that. He should have told her upfront that he'd planned on going to the Winchester estate. But he hadn't been using her, for God's sake.

Her accusations swirled around in his head with thoughts of that little kid.

He hadn't expected how seeing that boy would affect him. Technically, Declan was Carson's nephew—Josh was pretty sure, anyway. Sitting on a hospital bed and making it go up and down to keep the two-year-old from having a meltdown… It made him yearn for what he didn't have. And watching

Nora Winchester take the boy from him and cuddle him against her chest?

That, too, was something he yearned for. He and Sydney had been waiting. Always waiting. She had wanted her business to be more established and Josh's career to be more settled and...

He didn't have anything.

That wasn't true. He had good friends like the Newport boys, and he had his family—his grandfather and his brothers and sisters. He ran a successful business and he didn't want for anything.

Anything but a family of his own.

There were times when he just didn't want to do this anymore. It always hurt when people told him to get over Sydney's death, but getting over it and moving on were what he desperately wanted to do. He wanted to close the door on that part of his life and bolt it shut. He didn't want to leave it cracked open so that at random times—like right now—that never-ending sense of loss could barge in and catch him unaware.

It was past eleven by the time he pulled up in front of Lucy's apartment building. Somehow, the thought of going back to Carson's place and reporting on what he'd found at Sutton's felt like a mountain he'd never finish climbing. Because he didn't want to do this anymore, either—be the go-between for Carson and his sisters and their father. He wanted to go back to the nice, busy life he'd made for himself in Cedar

Point. There, at least, he didn't have Sydney's ghost waiting for him around every corner.

And after tonight he wasn't about to invite himself up to Lucy's place. He knew when to hold 'em and he knew when to fold 'em and, by God, he was going to fold tonight.

But she didn't get out of the truck. Lucy just sat there while the engine rumbled. Josh gave her twenty, thirty seconds and then figured that she didn't want to get out of the truck, so he turned the engine off and waited.

And they just sat there. She was looking straight ahead again, but she wasn't sitting ramrod straight anymore. She had her elbow on the truck door and her head leaned on her hand.

He knew that look. She was thinking—hard. So he let her think. Outside the truck, cars passed them and the occasional person walked down the sidewalk. She might tell him that she never wanted to see him again—but she might not.

He hoped not.

"We were so young," she said into the silence.

"When?" Because he was not going to make any assumptions whatsoever in the course of this conversation.

"When Gary died. I wasn't even eighteen."

Wait—was she still mad at him? It didn't sound like it. "It was a long time ago." Why was she bringing up Gary now? In all honesty, Josh hadn't thought that much about him after he'd gotten wrapped up

"FAST FIVE" READER SURVEY

Your participation entitles you to:

✳ 4 Thank-You Gifts Worth Over $20!

Complete the survey in minutes.

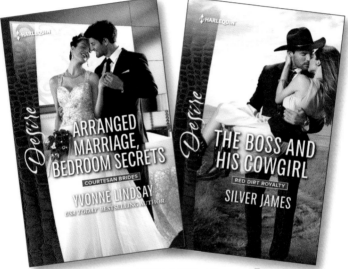

Get 2 FREE Books

See inside for details.

Dear Reader,

Since you are a lover of our books, your opinions are important to us... and so is your time.

That's why we made sure your **"FAST FIVE" READER SURVEY** can be completed in just a few minutes. Your answers to the five questions will help us remain at the forefront of women's fiction.

And, as a thank-you for participating, we'd like to send you **4 FREE THANK-YOU GIFTS!**

Enjoy your gifts with our appreciation,

Pam Powers

To get your
4 FREE THANK-YOU GIFTS:

✻ Quickly complete the "Fast Five" Reader Survey
and return the insert.

"FAST FIVE" READER SURVEY

1	Do you sometimes read a book a second or third time?	○ Yes ○ No
2	Do you often choose reading over other forms of entertainment such as television?	○ Yes ○ No
3	When you were a child, did someone regularly read aloud to you?	○ Yes ○ No
4	Do you sometimes take a book with you when you travel outside the home?	○ Yes ○ No
5	In addition to books, do you regularly read newspapers and magazines?	○ Yes ○ No

YES! I have completed the above Reader Survey. Please send me my 4 FREE GIFTS (gifts worth over $20 retail). I understand that I am under no obligation to buy anything, as explained on the back of this card.

225/326 HDL GKEU

FIRST NAME

LAST NAME

ADDRESS

APT.#

CITY

STATE/PROV.

ZIP/POSTAL CODE

with Sydney. Gary had become a bittersweet memory when Josh had chosen to think about him at all.

"Do you know," she said in a wistful voice, "that he was my first boyfriend?"

Josh sat up, instantly on alert. "That doesn't seem right."

"I didn't grow up in Cedar Point," she reminded him. "We moved so much—I know we never really talked about it, but my dad couldn't hold a job. I was surprised that I was able to stay in Cedar Point long enough to graduate. I was there for almost two whole years."

"But you were smart and cute." For the first time in a long time, she looked at him, even if it was only to roll her eyes. "I mean, in a tomboyish kind of way. You were fun."

"No, I wasn't. I've never had any sense of fashion or style, and have never been cute. I was a know-it-all—and an insufferable one, at that. We moved so much that I rarely had friends. Until you. You and Gary."

She was making herself sound like some sort of loser, which is not how he remembered her. "But we had fun together."

That got him a smile that was sad around the corners. "We did, didn't we? An insufferable know-it-all, the dying boy and you. The all-American boy next door."

He remembered something she'd said earlier, something that had hit him wrong. "I wasn't too good for you, you know." Really, if it hadn't been for the fact that Gary had been dying, who knew how it might have turned out? "But you were with Gary."

She sat up again, looking stiffer. "And you were his friend, first and foremost."

"I was. We'd been friends since kindergarten. There are some things a man doesn't do to his friend." Like steal his girl, for example.

Lucy was sort of bobbing her head, and Josh couldn't tell if she was agreeing with him or thinking hard. Or both.

Then she moved. She unbuckled her seat belt and turned to face him with her entire body. "Like what?"

The hairs on the back of Josh's arm stood up. "What do you mean?"

She scooted toward him on the old bench seat. "What are some things that a man doesn't do to his friend?"

Josh didn't answer. He wasn't sure he could find his voice, not with Lucy sliding toward him, an odd look in her eyes.

"Like what?" she repeated more softly. There was a note to her tone that hadn't been there earlier and Josh couldn't help but think that she knew what he was trying not to say.

"Why do we have to talk about this?"

"Because," she said, reaching out and tracing the line of his jaw with her fingertips, "I think I understand now."

"Understand what?" But he was already leaning

toward her, letting her pull him in closer. He had no idea what she was talking about, but he didn't care.

He simply did not care. He felt raw and exposed, as if someone had scraped off the top layer of his skin, and he didn't want to hurt anymore. He didn't want to think about his dead wife. He was tired of grief and sorrow, and he just wanted to get over it and he couldn't. He didn't know how.

Lucy was close enough to kiss now. Her breast brushed up against his arm and the warmth from her body calmed his raw nerves. "I understand." But she didn't kiss him and he wished like hell she would.

Because she was going to have to do it this time. There wasn't going to be any more confusion about this. If she wanted him, she had to come to him.

She tilted her head to one side and something in the air between them changed. "Will you come upstairs?"

"Lucy…" But already his body was responding to hers—her scent, her warmth. And what he really wanted was to go back to where they'd been earlier this evening. "If I come upstairs—"

"Stay," she whispered against his mouth. "Because I've missed you, too, Josh Calhoun."

It wasn't much of a kiss, the way her lips, light and sweet, brushed over his. It wasn't a kiss of passion or possession. But it was something else entirely— it was hopeful.

What the hell were they doing still sitting in the cab of his truck? Because he wasn't a teenager anymore—

getting it on in the vehicle no longer held any appeal. "I want to strip you out of those clothes and lay you out on that bed and I don't care who hears us," he told her as he wrenched off his seat belt.

"Yes," she hissed. "I want you on top of me, inside of me—oh, God, Josh."

Somehow, they got out of the truck and into the building. Josh pulled her into his arms and fell back against the wall next to the elevator. "You're really sure?" he asked, trying to convince himself that whatever she said would be okay.

"I've never wanted anything more in my life," she told him. And then she grabbed his butt. The feeling of her hands on his body did mighty interesting things to him. It had been so long...

He didn't want to think about that. Not right now. Instead, he wanted to figure out a way to make this night last for as long as possible.

He slid his hands over her body. She responded beautifully, arching into his touch and rubbing her breasts against his chest. But before he could do anything else, the elevator doors opened and Lucy dragged him inside.

There was an itch in the back of his mind, a question he didn't have the answer to. What did she understand?

But that question was buried under the sensation of Lucy pulling him down into her, Lucy digging her hands into his butt, Lucy moaning in his ear as he palmed her breast. "I want you so badly," she whispered as she raked her fingers through his hair and pulled his mouth to her.

Hell, that was all the permission he needed. He flattened her back against the wall of the elevator and hooked one leg over his hand, lifting her up so he could thrust against her.

"Oh, Josh," she moaned as her head fell back, exposing her neck. As he ground against her, he trailed his lips over her pale skin. "I want this shirt off you," he growled as he skimmed his teeth over the spot where her neck met her shoulders.

"Yes, yes," she panted as she clung to him.

Then the elevator dinged. Josh had to set her down and let her get her keys out, and the pause gave him back just enough self-control. He hadn't done this in a long time and he didn't want to screw it up. He wasn't under any illusions that this was going to be a regular thing, because she was in Chicago and after he left, he didn't know when he'd come back. He didn't know if he would come back for her.

So this had to count. It was so tempting to throw her on the bed and thrust into her until he came with mindless pleasure, but this was Lucy. She deserved more than that and he was going to give it to her.

"Sorry," she said, shooting him a guilty look over her shoulder as she fumbled with her keys.

He leaned down and put his lips against the back of her neck. "Nervous?" As he asked this, he settled his hands on her hips and began rubbing small circles with his thumbs.

She shrugged and got the door open. "Maybe a little."

He followed her inside, unwilling to break the physical connection. "We'll take it slow. I want to make this so good for you." He kicked the door shut behind him and leaned against it, pulling her back into him. His arms went around her waist and he just held her.

The feeling of her body against his—he had missed this. Five years of sleeping alone, of taking care of his own needs quickly—it hadn't been about pleasure. It hadn't been about want and need and another person. He almost wanted to laugh. Because for the first time in years, he didn't feel the crushing loneliness. And that was thanks to Lucy.

"It's all right," she said in a soft voice as she reached up and slid a hand behind his neck.

Of course, it was all right—everything about this was just *fine*. Still, her words had an oddly reassuring effect on him and he hugged her even tighter. Then he began to move. Because a man couldn't get lucky if he stood by the door all night long. He splayed his hands over her ribs and began to stroke up, then down. "I want to take this off."

"Please do," she said, and underneath his lips, he could feel the pulse in her neck begin to beat faster.

He skimmed his hands up over her breasts to the buttons of her shirt. Slowly, he undid one and then the next until the entire shirt was open and he could slip his hands underneath. Her skin was warm to the touch—and touch it he did. He trailed his fingertips over her waist, over the smooth front of her bra. The whole time he stroked her, he kept his lips against her pulse and listened to her breath in his ear.

He wanted to make this all about her. Because this was Lucy. If all he cared about was getting laid, he could've accomplished that easily at any point in the last five years.

But he didn't just want to get off. He missed making love.

So that's what he was doing tonight. He was going to make love to Lucy with everything he had. They didn't have to worry about dating and that awkward getting-to-know-you period, and they didn't have to worry about long-term relationships. He already knew Lucy and he already liked her and he already loved making her gasp in that little way she was doing as he stroked her nipples with his fingertips.

"You like that, don't you?" he asked as he felt her nipples stiffen under his touch. He began lightly pinching them.

"Oh, Josh," she whimpered as he teased her flesh.

"Yeah, that's it, babe." One part of his brain wanted to remember that Sydney had always liked it when he played with her breasts, too, but he pushed that away. His wife was gone and he wanted to believe with all his heart that she would want him to do this. She would want him to grab a little bit of happiness, even if it was only for one night. Sydney would want him to find a piece of himself again with an old friend whom he could trust.

He relinquished Lucy's left breast and began to slide his hand lower, over the soft planes of her stomach and then down over the front of her pants. She sagged back against him and he was happy to carry her weight. Earlier, on the couch, he had just wanted to make her come. It had almost been as though he *needed* to make her come to prove that he hadn't forgotten how. But now he wanted this to be slow and sweet and so good that neither of them ever wanted it to end.

Her breathing got more labored as he rubbed slow circles against her sex. She clutched at his arms with her hands and shifted against him, the pressure of her bottom against his erection pushing any rational thought from his mind. This was what he wanted— not thinking, just doing. Just feeling.

Suddenly, she gasped and her fingernails dug into his arm. "Bed," she ordered. "Now."

"Yes, ma'am." He half turned her and leaned down so he could sweep her into his arms. She'd always been a small thing.

"Josh!" she squeaked as he settled her against his chest.

He grinned down at her. Her cheeks were flushed, her pupils dilated wide—so wide, he almost couldn't see the blue in her eyes anymore. "I've got you," he reassured her as he carried her into the bedroom and over to the bed. He found the gap in the sheer curtain she'd hung around it and pushed it open. He sat her down on the bed and got rid of those doctor shoes she was wearing. Her socks quickly followed and then he took his time peeling her shirt off her arms.

"Look at you," he said, his voice wavering as he stared down at her. Her bra was what Sydney had always called serviceably beige—a plain beige. It wasn't all that sexy—but on Lucy? "I don't remember you having this body back in high school." He knelt on the bed so he could undo the bra.

"I didn't," she said, angling her body so he didn't have to stretch as far. "I was the definition of a late bloomer."

Josh was out of practice, so it took three tries before the bra hooks gave successfully. He tossed the bra to the side. "Wow, Lucy, your breasts were worth the wait."

Because they were fabulous—full and rounded and high on her chest. He fell to his knees before her and just took a moment to appreciate the beauty that was the female body.

She reached over and started working the buttons on his shirt. "Your turn," she said as she began to strip him.

She got his shirt off, but when she went for his jeans he pushed her hands out of the way. "Patience." He didn't know if he was admonishing her or himself.

"I'm tired of being patient," she told him. "You have no idea how long I've been waiting for this."

He thought she was going to say something else,

so he cut her off the only way he knew how—he leaned down and wrapped his lips around her nipple. He sucked her into his mouth and was rewarded with a ragged gasp of pleasure. She threaded her fingers into his hair again and held him against her.

He was so hard in his jeans that it was becoming physically painful. He wasn't going to last. All of his good intentions about laying her out and making her scream were not going to amount to a hill of beans if he couldn't find a little more restraint.

But he couldn't help it. God, she felt so good in his mouth, under his hands. "Oh, Josh," she kept repeating as he sucked and licked and nibbled at first one breast, then the other. Somehow he managed to get the button and zipper of her pants undone. Reluctantly, he relinquished the hold he had on her nipples and laid her back on the bed so he could get her pants off.

As he stared down at her, he had a weird feeling of being out of time—that this was something that should've always happened, but the timing just hadn't been right.

"God, Lucy" was all he could say as he peeled her panties off her, and then she lay bare before him. Something clicked in his mind, and one word popped to the front of his consciousness.

Mine.

"I don't know how you think we're going to have sex if you stand there and stare at me all night," she said with what he hoped was an ironic smile. She lifted her foot and nudged his crotch. "And we're going to have sex—right?"

The next thing he knew, Josh was stripping out of his jeans and kicking off his boots—and coming to a dead halt. *Oh, no.*

"Josh?" Lucy pushed herself up and stared at him with new concern on her face.

"I don't have anything," he said in a shaky voice. "I didn't plan on this—I don't have any condoms." And he was no longer some stupid kid who could talk himself out of using one because "nothing would happen." He absolutely would not risk Lucy's health and safety with an accidental pregnancy just because he wanted to get laid for the first time in five years.

"Oh." Everything about her wilted. But then she perked up again. "Wait!" She threw herself off the bed and hurried to what Josh assumed was the closet. She hauled out a huge blue duffel bag and crouched down—which provided Josh with one hell of a view of her backside—as she rifled through it. "I think—oh, thank God." She stood up and turned around, holding three small foil squares in her hand. "I keep a fully stocked medical kit—for emergencies," she said, suddenly looking shy again. "You never know."

"I think this qualifies as an emergency," Josh told her. His erection heartily agreed.

She looked so innocent with that little grin on her face. "Will this be enough?"

That made Josh laugh out loud. "Babe, I'm not eighteen anymore." He took the condoms from her and pulled her into his arms again. As he kissed her, he realized that they fit together. God, it felt so good to hold her.

He lifted her up and laid her on the bed. Later, there would be time for niceties like oral sex and lots of foreplay. Right now, he couldn't wait—not a minute longer. He knelt between her knees and tore open one of the condom packets. She stared at him as he rolled it on. "Okay?" he asked.

"Okay," she said breathlessly. "I never..."

He leaned over her and reached down between her legs. She was wet to the touch, so ready for him. "I never thought this would happen, either. But I'm so glad it is. Lucy, you have no idea how glad."

She bucked at his touch and threw her arms around his neck. "Me, too," she whispered as he positioned himself against her.

Slowly—as slowly as he could manage—he began to thrust into her.

Very slowly.

Too slowly.

"Don't stop," she said, clinging to him. Something wasn't right, but before Josh could ask her—maybe they did need to take the time for some oral sex—she kissed him, hard, while pulling him down into her. "Now," she demanded. "*Now*, Josh."

Her body gave a little against him and her fingernails dug into his back, pushing him forward. With a grunt, he sank into her. The feeling of her wet warmth surrounding him, taking him in—it short-circuited something in his brain. She moaned as her back arched and Josh couldn't hold himself back anymore.

He gave himself up to the sensations. Everything he had he gave to her. At one point, her nails bit into him so deeply that he had to grab her wrists and hold them over her head. "Oh, God, Josh," she whispered in a high, tight voice as she moved underneath him, rising up to meet him over and over again.

"You like that, don't you?" he asked as he stroked into her. He held both of her wrists with one hand and propped himself up so he could drive in deeper. "You like it hard like that, don't you?"

"Yes," she whimpered, her head thrashing from side to side as he buried himself in her body. "Make me come, Josh," she begged.

They were pretty, sweet words—and he hadn't known how much he needed to hear them until Lucy said them. He couldn't let go until she went first. Somehow he was able to shift so that he still had a hold of her wrists but he was sitting farther back on his knees so he could reach down between her legs and stroke his thumb over her clit. It didn't take much pressure—a few gentle strokes timed with a few hard thrusts—and her head came up off the pillow, her mouth open as she completely came apart.

Josh fought against the urge to let go. Instead, he forced himself to take in every memory of this moment. This was what he hadn't gotten on the couch earlier—the sight of Lucy letting go.

He'd done that. He'd given that to her. He still could.

It was nothing compared to what she was giving him.

It was only when her orgasm had passed and she'd fallen back on the pillow, panting, that Josh followed her over the edge. He leaned forward and kissed her hard as he pumped two, three more times. And then he came. The sweet release, her body surrounding him—God, he'd missed so much. *So* much.

He fell onto her and rolled off, not wanting to crush her. When he released her wrists, she threw her arms around him and held him tight. They didn't say anything.

What was there to say? He didn't know. He didn't have any words right now.

Finally, he pulled away and rolled out of bed. "I'll be right back," he said. It was then—and only then—that he glanced down and saw the blood.

Nine

"What the—*Lucy*?"

Something in Josh's tone made Lucy open her eyes. She didn't want to. She wanted to pull him back into her arms and curl around his chest—God, what a chest—and drift off into sleep. She wanted to wake up that way, too, and then she wanted him to hold her down again and make mad passionate love to her again and again and *again*.

She met his gaze and then he looked down at his penis. So she looked, too. She was allowed to look. They were lovers now and lovers got to openly stare at each other's naked bodies whenever they wanted, right?

That wasn't all she was looking at. It wasn't his manhood—it was the bloodstained condom.

And reality—that cruel, heartless bitch—came intruding into her happy dream.

"You were a virgin?" He asked in the same tone of voice he might use to ask if Bigfoot really existed.

Was there any good way to have this conversation? No. But there had to be a better way than this.

"Um," she started, and then stopped because that wasn't any sort of answer at all. "Yes?" She winced at the way it came out as a question. Because she knew it wasn't.

His eyes narrowed and he put his hands on his hips. "I'll be right back," he told her. "And then you and I are going to have a talk."

Without waiting for an answer, he turned and stalked away. Normally, she would've taken advantage of this opportunity to admire his butt. It was at that exact moment that she began to feel the effects of her first time. She was sore and stretched and her labia burned. Despite all that, she wanted him back in her bed again.

She sat up in bed, wincing as her delicate parts came into contact with the sheet. And then she winced again because there was probably more blood. She felt different—and that was an understatement. But at the same time, she didn't feel as different as she'd thought she would. She'd gained some firsthand knowledge—but she didn't think it had fundamentally altered who she was. She wasn't a virgin anymore, but she still felt like Lucy. She'd climaxed—two climaxes in one night wasn't bad for a first timer—but the heavens hadn't opened and the angels hadn't sung and she hadn't heard any fireworks go off.

She rubbed her temples. Being different and not different at the same time made her feel funny.

The bathroom door opened and Josh strode out. This was the stuff of fantasy, she had to admit. Because she had fantasized about this many times, except in her fantasies, Josh had always been leaner, more gangly. More awkward. He'd been the teenager she remembered.

He hadn't been this broad, muscled man with a sprinkling of dark chest hair. He also hadn't been this intimidating man with his jaw set and his eyes hard.

Before she could think of anything reasonable to say, he told her, "Your turn."

Lucy took the hint. She went to the bathroom and got cleaned up and then looked at herself in the mirror. She looked the way she felt—different and the same. Her hair was a disaster and her cheeks were flushed and her lips were red. She looked as though she had taken a lover. But she didn't look like a different woman. A more mature, more sophisticated version of herself was not staring back at her.

And now she had to go out and "have a talk" with Josh about this whole pesky virginity thing.

Was sex always this complicated?

She turned off the light before she opened the door, as if that would hide her. It didn't.

She saw that Josh had put his briefs back on, but

nothing else. He was sitting on the edge of her bed, his forearms on his legs, and for the life of her, Lucy thought that he looked like he was praying. Oh, this was going to be bad, wasn't it? This was going to be complicated and messy and awkward and painful, and it was going to be all the worse because she didn't know how to have these conversations.

"Explain to me," Josh said in a low voice that bordered on dangerous, "how you were still a virgin." He didn't look up as she approached. He kept his head bowed and his gaze focused on the floor, on his toes or some imaginary speck of dust.

"I've been busy." That got his attention. His head popped up and he stared at her, and Lucy had a fleeting impression of...guilt? "Well, I have been. You don't get to be the youngest head of oncology in a hospital by having a social life."

She felt awkward standing before him, but she figured it would be even more awkward if she went and sat next to him. She looked around and saw her bathrobe on the floor near her closet. She must have launched it there when she was frantically trying to get packed earlier. She bent over and flipped it over her shoulders, belting it at the waist. Immediately, she felt less exposed.

"But that doesn't make any sense." He didn't remark on her bathrobe. At least it was a nice plain white bathrobe—not a fluffy penguin in sight.

"Yes, it does." Something in his eyes shifted. Instead of guilt, it looked more like he might feel sorry for her. And Lucy couldn't have that. "After high school, I wasn't exactly looking for another relationship. I threw myself into my studies. I got my BA in three years. Then there was med school and internships and residencies and…and my patients. I didn't make time for dating and I didn't have a lot of offers, so it worked out. I have my job and that's all I need."

Or it had been until Josh Calhoun had walked back into her life. Now? Now she wasn't so sure anymore.

And that, more than the loss of her virginity, was what had changed about her. Because Lucinda Wilde had been a doctor who hadn't needed a personal relationship, who had convinced herself that she didn't even want one.

But Lucy Wilde?

Josh stood and paced away from her. "No, that *doesn't* make any sense," he repeated with more authority. "What about you and Gary?"

This was always what it was going to come back to, wasn't it? No matter what curveballs life had thrown at them—and this sure as hell counted as a curveball—it would always begin back where it started.

"What about us?" She shifted from foot to foot, trying to find the posture that took a little more pressure off her newly sore parts.

"You guys were together—I mean, you dated for, like, two years!"

Lucinda Wilde, MD, would have stayed standing to make her best argument. But Lucy was tired. It was after midnight, and she had to get up tomorrow and keep dealing with Sutton Winchester and everyone else. So she sat on the bed and tried her best to keep from yawning. "And Gary was sick, Josh. I know that you guys were friends from childhood, but when I showed up at school, he was already sick. I never knew him when he was healthy."

He spun and stared at her. "What are you saying?"

She shrugged. "I wish I could tell you that we didn't go all the way because we were waiting for the right time or we thought he would get better and we'd get married or we knew we weren't mature enough to deal with it. But the truth was, he was sick."

She didn't want to tell Josh the rest. She wanted to let that part of Gary stay buried. But she knew, just from looking at Josh's face, that she wasn't going to be able to do that. She sent up a silent prayer for forgiveness to Gary's spirit, wherever he was.

"But he loved you," Josh said. He sounded so young and idealistic—as if he really did believe love could cure the world of all its ills. Lucy couldn't help but smile. "And you loved him—didn't you?"

"I did. He was a good kisser—not that I had anything to compare him to—and we fooled around. Just because I was a virgin didn't mean I've never done anything. The spirit was willing but his flesh was... weak." No matter how hard she'd tried, Gary Everly had died a virgin in the strictest sense of the word.

She wanted that to be the end of it. "Will you stay with me? I'm tired, Josh."

He took two steps toward her and then stopped. Lucy braced herself because she knew it was coming and she knew she couldn't stop it. "You—after Gary's funeral when you kissed me—what was *that* about, then?" He looked horrified.

She tried to smile, as if they were reminiscing about lighthearted tales of frivolity instead of life-and-death issues. "Why did you kiss me tonight? Earlier, after you told me about your wife?" His mouth opened and then he shut it again. "Why did you come upstairs with me tonight—after you played with that little boy?"

The color drained out of his face and he looked as if she'd slapped him. Hard.

She stood up and walked over to him, laying her palm against his cheek. "I understand," she told him gently.

For a moment, she thought he was going to give. His arms twitched as if he wanted to pull her tight against his chest. And that was what she wanted.

But that was not what happened. "Did you—did you just have *pity sex* with me? Is that what that was? You give up your virginity after all these years to make me feel better about my dead wife?" His voice had risen until he had shouted that last part.

She stumbled back. "No! That's not what this was, Josh!"

"Then what was it?"

"I *like* you," she told him, trying to keep the panic out of her voice. This was not how it was supposed to go. Even a novice like herself knew that. "I've always liked you. And I thought—after you explicitly told me—that you liked me, too!"

"Jesus, Lucy." He pushed past her and started gathering up his clothes.

Now she was panicking in earnest. "What are you doing?"

"Leaving," he told her shortly as he shoved his legs into his pants and then his feet into his boots. "This was a mistake. God, what was I thinking?"

That did it. Some of her panic flipped over into anger. "Boy, you sure know how to make a girl feel special, don't you? Just what every virgin wants to hear, that she was nothing but a mistake. Would you just listen to me? This wasn't pity sex!"

He jammed his arms into his shirt and didn't even bother to button it up. "Wasn't it?" He made a break for the door. She grabbed his arm and tried to hold him still. "A thirty-five-year-old virgin and a widower and you're going to tell me that's not pitiful?"

She gasped in shock, humiliation blossoming in her chest. "I am not pitiful," she said, her voice shaking with anger. "And neither are you."

He cut her a mean look and opened his mouth. She tensed, but he didn't say anything. Instead, he spun on his heel and walked right out of her apartment.

All she could do was watch him go.

And that?

That was pitiful.

Ten

Somehow, Josh found himself outside Carson's place. He didn't get out of the truck immediately; instead, he sat there, fighting the urge to bash his forehead against the steering wheel in frustration.

What had just happened? He found himself repeating that question over and over again—not that repeating it got him any closer to an answer.

He had slept with Lucy. She had been a virgin. Those facts were just that—facts.

It was also a fact that he had—and this was an understatement—flipped out. And the hell of it was, he had no idea why. Not one single idea. But he was pretty damn sure that in the process of flipping out he had grievously insulted Lucy. Which just made everything that much worse.

He had screwed up. That was bad enough. Technically, he'd screwed up twice. Basically, his evening with Lucy had had three stages—plumbing the depths of his grief, seducing her and insulting her.

Only one of those had been any fun. And he'd screwed that up, too.

It was well past one when Josh finally dragged himself into the house. He was surprised to find all three Newport brothers sitting in a parlor. For a moment, he had a flashback to high school, of trying to sneak in past his curfew only to find his grandfather sitting up and waiting for him.

But he wasn't in high school anymore and nobody was going to ground him. The first person to try was going to get a fat lip for his troubles.

Here they all sat, each one of them looking at him expectantly. Because he had been assigned a task—go to the Winchester estate and make sure that Sutton Winchester would be well cared for in a private setting.

And, idiot that he was, he had used Lucy for that purpose.

"We were beginning to wonder where you'd gotten off to," Graham said in a diplomatic tone. Before Josh could tell him exactly where he could go, Graham added, "Whiskey?" as he held up his own tumbler. It was mostly empty.

Yeah, he could use a drink. But he was in no mood

to drink in present company. "Lucy has given her approval of the setup. She's waiting on one set of test results and then she'll discharge him."

Brooks rolled his eyes, Graham threw back the rest of his drink and Carson sat forward, looking interested.

"Anything else?" Carson asked.

Josh had always been a peacemaker. Ever since he'd buried his parents, he'd had to be. His grandfather had leaned on him in his time of sorrow. His brothers and sisters had needed him to step up, especially after his elder brother, Lincoln, had joined the military and bailed on them. His employees had disputes that needed settling. Even his friends—the Newports especially—had been well served by Josh's calm, steady presence.

And he was tired of it.

"The estate is lovely. Your sister Nora is a sweet soul. Your nephew Declan is adorable."

"Problem?" Graham asked, reaching over for a crystal decanter to refill his glass. "Are you sure you don't want some whiskey?"

"No, damn it, I don't want any whiskey."

Brooks snorted. "What crawled up your butt and died?" he asked, and Josh thought he seemed to be enjoying himself a little too much.

Josh glared at him—at them all. "You're just waiting for him to die. Can't you let a man die in peace?"

Brooks shrugged. "He doesn't even deserve that much, you know. I'd have tossed him on the street if I could." Brooks glanced at Carson and muttered a halfhearted, "Sorry."

"No, you're not," Josh snapped. "You're hell-bent on this vendetta." He turned to Graham. "I haven't figured out what your angle is yet, but I know you too well to know you're *not* working on an angle."

Carson ignored this outburst. "You agreed that moving him was a good idea. In fact, you're the one who convinced me it might get him to talk."

"Of course I did. I was keeping the damn peace. I always keep the peace." Except tonight. Except with Lucy. God, what a mess. He felt like his skin was turning inside out. It was too much. He never should have come back to Chicago. "The next time you want to find out what's happening at your father's house, go there yourself. In the meantime, stop expecting me to do your dirty work. Because now Lucy has to rearrange her entire life so that she can coddle a man no one else wants to coddle."

The three brothers exchanged knowing—and irritating—looks. "Who is Lucy, again?" Brooks asked.

Carson stared at Josh. "Dr. Lucinda Wilde. Sutton's oncologist—and apparently a former old friend of Josh's." There was a pause while Brooks and Graham digested this information, and then Carson added, "Or perhaps, she's not that former a friend."

"Go to hell," Josh retorted. "I am *your* friend. You want advice? Fine. You want to talk about it? Fine. But I'm not your errand boy and I'm not your employee—

not anymore. I didn't come back to Chicago for the first time in five long, dark years just so you could use me and Lucy to fight some proxy battle. If you can't get that—any of you—then I'll be gone by morning. I have a business to run."

He turned and started to stalk out of the room, but Carson called after him, "Josh?"

He stopped at the doorway, but he didn't turn back around. "What?"

"We know it wasn't easy for you to come back. But we're glad you did."

"Whatever." And then Josh did something that was normally uncharacteristic of him—but something he'd done twice tonight, nevertheless.

He walked away without looking back.

"What's wrong with you?"

Lucy startled and glanced up from her tablet. Sutton Winchester was a man who looked sick. Ever since they'd started chemo and radiation, his skin had taken on a sickly gray pall. He'd lost a lot of weight and all of his hair in a very short period of time, which gave him a nearly skeletal appearance.

But Lucy saw reasons for hope. He was able to keep some food down and the last scan of his lungs has shown that the tumor appeared to be shrinking.

"Sorry?"

Sutton sighed and repeated himself. "What's wrong with you? Somebody die? Wasn't me, was it?" That last bit he wheezed out.

"No, actually. Nothing's wrong. Your numbers are looking good and I think we're starting to see your tumor shrink."

Sutton's head was propped up on the pillows, and he seemed so weak that he could barely keep his eyes open at half-mast. But appearances, she knew, could be deceiving, and she got the feeling that Sutton was watching her far more closely than he should be. "You look like somebody dumped you," he went on. "I've got three daughters. I know these things."

Great. Just what she needed. "Mr. Winchester, not that it's relevant to your treatment, but I'm not seeing anyone. Ergo, no one can dump me."

Sutton's eyes drifted shut and she hoped that maybe he was going to fall asleep. But today was not her lucky day. "Someone sent you flowers— the nurses were talking about it. You're too good for him."

This wasn't exactly an unknown phenomenon. Sometimes, when people were facing death, they became more philosophical about the trials and tribulations of life. Those regrets were then projected onto those around them. If they'd been neglectful parents, they would cajole and beg the nurses and doctors to take better care of their own families. If they'd been unfaithful, they would talk of love and honor and respect, of vows they hadn't kept and now wished they had.

Just her luck that Sutton Winchester would fall into more than one of those categories. "Mr. Winchester," she began in a stern tone. "My personal life has no bearing on your treatment—and that's the thing that you and I should both be concerned with at this time. Your family has gone to great lengths to have you transferred out of this hospital and returned to your home."

Sutton cracked open one eye and Lucy thought maybe he looked a little alarmed. "What? Why?"

"They want me to continue your treatment at home, where you will have greater control over your privacy."

His other eye opened and he stared at her. "You're not sending me home to die, are you?"

"No. I'm not giving up on you and you should not give up, either. In fact," she went on, staring at her tablet and nothing in particular, "I'm going to be living at the estate in the room next to yours for the time being so that I can ensure that you're receiving the best care possible twenty-four hours a day."

Sutton didn't respond immediately. She couldn't tell if this announcement surprised or pleased him— or made him furious. Finally, he said, "You don't come cheap, I assume?"

No, but the fact that she was selling her services to the highest bidder had a way of making her feel pretty damned cheap. "The Newports and the Winchesters have generously agreed to provide the bulk of the funding for the new cancer pavilion expansion here at Midwest."

Sutton exhaled and seemed to sink back into his

pillows. The conversation had clearly worn him out. "Should've held out for more," he said in a tone of voice that would've been scolding if he'd had any energy. "You need to be a tougher negotiator."

"Yes, well, you and I are going to have a lot of time together over the next several weeks. I look forward to hearing how you would recommend I go about doing just that."

She watched him for a moment longer, but he'd settled in to sleep.

As she walked out of Sutton's room, she almost ran into John Jackson, the vice president of the hospital. "Dr. Wilde! Just the person I was hoping to see!" he gushed.

Lucy didn't necessarily believe in a sixth sense, but if she had one, hers was telling her to run. Quickly. "Mr. Jackson, how can I help you today?"

"I wanted to be the one to tell you," he went on, grinning like a loon. "It's simply wonderful!"

She began to back away from him. "I already know about the cancer pavilion," she reminded him.

"No, no! I mean, well—yes. This is about the cancer pavilion. Sort of."

"Mr. Jackson," Lucy said, pinching the bridge of her nose under her glasses. "I'm making my rounds—if you could be so kind as to get to the point?"

"Yes, yes—of course. The Newports are hosting a gala benefit for the children's hospital they're building."

She stared at him because that wasn't exactly news. Nor was it relevant to her. "So?"

"So!" He clapped his hands. "They want you to be the guest of honor!"

Oh, God. "Why?"

"Why?" Jackson blinked at her. "It's because of everything you're doing for them. This is wonderful! The publicity—the visibility!"

Lucy could feel all eyes from the nurses station on her. Her life was no longer her own and everyone knew it. She did her best to put on a brave face, though. "How delightful. And when are the festivities scheduled?"

"Three weeks!" Jackson was physically bouncing on the balls of his feet, which made him look like a four-year-old who was so excited about a birthday present he couldn't stand still. "I'm sure we can make time for you to attend—what with you being the guest of honor and all."

Translation? This was not an optional event. Attendance was mandatory.

She remembered what Sutton had said to her just a few minutes ago. "And what are we going to get out of it?" There. That was her being a better negotiator.

Jackson's smile cracked, but Lucy was done with the social niceties. They never got her anywhere, anyway. "It will be a fund-raising event. With the Winchesters and the Newports hosting, the cream of Chicago's high society will be in attendance."

If she was going to give up yet another part of

her life—and her self-determination—she needed to
make sure it was for a greater cause. She wanted to
tell Jackson that the children's hospital should have
the best damned children's oncology department in
the country—but she knew that Jackson was only
concerned with Midwest. "That cardiac cath lab you
wanted—I won't go unless we get a commitment of
funds for that," she told Jackson.

"Yes, well, yes," Jackson blustered, as if the idea
of an oncologist caring about cardiology was so foreign as to be hilarious. "I'll see what I can do."

As much as Lucy wanted to hide in her office, she
was doing rounds. So she forced herself to nod at the
nurses who were busy *not* eavesdropping before she
went in to see her next patient, Mr. Gadhavi.

There was nothing good about this. She was so
well-known for her lack of a social life that the appearance of flowers had the entire department gos-
siping. She was so unpracticed at being dumped—if
you could call two almost-dates with Josh "dating"—
that even an old cad like Sutton Winchester could
tell that she was upset. And now she was going to
have to get dressed up and go to the benefit and smile
for all the people who were making her miserable.

Well, not all of them. With any luck, Josh Calhoun
would not be at the benefit.

She wanted so badly to blame this on Josh, but it
wasn't his fault—not entirely. Lucy had made herself a promise that she would not humiliate herself in

front of Josh again, and yet she'd managed that not once but twice in the course of a few hours.

Worse than the embarrassment—worse than having her virginity thrown back in her face—was that she hadn't seen his parting insult coming. Long ago, she'd stopped thinking of her sexual status as something to be pitied, condemned or fixed. It was a nonissue to her. Sure, she wished she dated. She wanted someone to come home to, someone to do things with. She wanted someone in her bed in the morning and at night. She wanted to love someone and she wanted to know that she was lovable.

But, ultimately, that was not how Josh had made her feel. When it came down to it, all of her choices, her hopes, her dreams—they had all been reduced to one simple label.

Thirty-five-year-old virgin.

And now she wasn't even that anymore.

She never wanted to see Josh Calhoun again.

The following days passed in a blur. Lucy packed up and relocated to the Winchester state. Sutton Winchester was discharged and transported home. When he had some energy, he complained loudly about the color of the walls, the remote for the TV that his daughters had picked out, the noises of the machines. When he was tired, he yelled or snipped or tried to browbeat Lucy and her nurses.

Lucy was pulling eight- to ten-hour days at Midwest. Then she would spend a couple of hours taking care of her personal business before she went to the Winchester estate and spent hours with Sutton Winchester or his daughters. Then she would sleep poorly, get up and do it all over again the next day.

She did not hear from Josh. Which was fine. She didn't want to.

Carson Newport came by to see his father on a regular basis—although the older man did not seem any more inclined now to answer Carson's questions than he had been when in the hospital.

Sutton's daughters stopped by to see him often, too. And they made sure that Lucy had anything she could possibly need. Staying at the Winchester estate was almost like being at a spa retreat—a working spa retreat, but still. Sutton's chef was excellent, Lucy's minifridge was well-stocked with soda and wine—not that she drank a lot while she was on call, which was all the time, but still—and a maid made up her room every day. In all honesty, it was as close to a vacation as she had gotten in years. Except for the man fighting for his life next door, that was.

Except for the fact that she didn't hear from Josh.

She'd been at the Winchester estate for six nights when she came home to find Carson sitting by Sutton's bed. They weren't talking, but Lucy got the feeling that Sutton was only pretending to be asleep. "How are we tonight?" she asked, wanting nothing more than a good soak in the enormous two-person whirlpool tub that was in her bathroom and knowing she couldn't. Not yet.

Carson stood and, with a glance back at his father, went to meet her in the doorway. "Is he always this quiet, or is he just avoiding talking to me?"

She thought she saw Sutton turn his head slightly at the sound of Carson's voice.

"Well…" she hedged. Her first priority was, as always, her patient. "The alternative seems to be yelling. Lots of yelling." The light in the room was dim, but she was almost positive she saw the corner of Sutton's mouth curve up. That old man wasn't fooling anyone right now.

Anyone except for Carson. "Dr. Wilde," he said in an even quieter voice, which made her lean in. "I wanted to apologize to you."

Lucy took a step back. "Why? Have you done something else that's going to…" She let her voice trail off because there was no way she could complete that sentence while maintaining a polite, professional exterior.

"I wanted to tell you that I appreciate everything you've done on behalf of our family. You've gone above and beyond the call of duty—you and Josh."

Lucy stiffened at the mention of Josh's name. "Oh? What else have you had him doing?"

A muscle in Carson's jaw clenched. "Nothing, actually. He's been back in Iowa for a week. I get the feeling that he's not talking to us. Me and my brothers," he quickly corrected. "I asked him to come with you last week to make sure the room was acceptable. As I understand it, that was not the best way to handle the situation and I put both of you in an uncomfortable position."

Lucy could feel all of the blood draining out of her face, but she did her level best not to have any other reaction. "Yes, well." That seemed to be the only thing she was capable of saying.

It should not matter that Josh had returned to Cedar Point without telling her. Why would it? He'd shown up in Chicago without letting her know, after all. He was under no obligation to keep her apprised of his movements. But, somehow, the fact that he'd not only walked out of her apartment without a look back but walked away from Chicago just stung all the more.

She really did mean that little to him. And that wasn't just an observation about the sex and the aftermath. Their years of friendship and their bond over Gary—it actually hadn't meant that much at all.

She must not have gotten any better recently at hiding her emotions, because Carson gave her a worried look and then gestured for her to step out into the hallway. He closed the door behind them. "I really am sorry," he said again.

Lucy tried to wave this away. "He mentioned that you guys were old friends. I understand how those things go."

Carson gave her an odd look. "Did something happen? If he was a jerk, I can go beat him up for you."

She lifted an eyebrow at him. "That won't be necessary." But her curiosity got the better of her. "You knew his wife, didn't you?"

"Sydney? Yes. We all loved her. It was funny how it shook out. I think Graham was actually interested in her when he introduced her to Josh. It was the sort of thing that could have ended a friendship. But Josh was the peacemaker."

"Yeah, he's always been that way." Except when it came to her, apparently. No, that wasn't fair. When they were around other people, it was fine. It was only when it was the two of them alone. That was when it all went to hell.

Carson seemed to consider this. "Have you ever seen him mad?"

"Of course," she said, trying not to think about the way things had ended. "Why?"

Carson ran a hand through his hair. "Because after he came back from here the other week, he was mad at us and told us to stop jerking you around. Not in so many words, but the message was the same."

Lucy tried to synthesize this information without actually reacting to it. "Yet the very next day, I was informed I would be a guest of honor at a gala banquet—instead of being asked."

Carson winced. "It wasn't my fault. That was entirely the doing of my sisters."

Lucy sighed. "It's fine."

She didn't mean it and she was pretty sure that Carson knew it. "If there's anything I can do to make it up to you…" he said.

"That won't be necessary." God only knew how he might try. "Now if you'll excuse me, I have a patient to attend."

Carson stepped aside and she moved past him. But against her better judgment, she paused with her hand on the doorknob. "If you do talk to Josh," she said, "could you make sure he's doing all right?"

Which was an admission of failure and she knew it. If she were really Josh's friend, she should be able to ask him that herself.

But she couldn't.

Carson nodded. "Yeah, I can do that."

Lucy managed to muster a wan smile and then went in to see her patient, closing the door behind her.

Sutton wasn't pretending to be asleep anymore. "You're back again," he said in the tone of voice that suggested he had a little more energy today. Which meant he was going to be cranky and Lucy was going to take the brunt of it. "Who is this Josh?"

"So you're feeling better," Lucy said, determined not to give him anything more to work with.

"I don't want you here anymore," Sutton snapped at her. "I want all these tubes out. I'm not that sick."

Lucy gave him a stern look, but the old man didn't even blink. "Did you chase Jenelle off?" she asked, looking around for the nurse who was supposed to be on duty.

"Carson told her to go get something to eat," Sutton grumbled. He lay back against the pillow and closed his eyes. "He looks so much like his mother."

Lucy did not want to be drawn into the Newport/ Winchester family drama any more than she had to be—but right now she'd rather deal with their drama than her own. "Have you told him that?"

Sutton didn't answer. Apparently, he was going to pretend to be asleep to any question he didn't feel like answering.

"Did you know your children are hosting a gala benefit for the new children's hospital the Newports are building? And I'm the guest of honor?"

That got his attention. "Why are they doing that?"

"Because I haven't killed you yet," she told him briskly. "And I took your advice—I negotiated for the cardiac cath lab funding at Midwest in exchange for being dressed up and paraded around like a trophy. Indirectly, you're helping a great many people who can't afford this level of care on their own—you know that, right?" She shot a snarky smile at him. "You might even get Humanitarian of the Year at the rate you're going."

When he didn't answer, she peeked at him again, expecting to find him asleep. But he was watching her closely. "This Josh was a fool to let you go."

She cringed. "Mr. Winchester, does this constitute flirting for you?"

That got the old man to grin. He still looked terrible—two steps above death warmed over—but grinning was an improvement. Laughter was the best medicine, after all. "If I were a stronger man, I'd have you on my arm at this benefit. And in my bed afterward." The smile still on his face, his eyes started to drift shut, and this time Lucy was sure that he wasn't faking sleep. His chest rose and fell in even breaths and a little color was coming back into his cheeks. It wouldn't last—this next round of chemo was due to hit tomorrow morning and he was going to look only one step above death warmed over then. But he hadn't given up.

Jenelle came back in, and she and Lucy conferred over Sutton's status.

When this was all over and Lucy went back to her normal life, she was sure she would feel like herself again. But that wasn't going to happen anytime soon.

She had a gala benefit she needed to get ready for, a patient to save and a hospital administrator to keep in line—not to mention all of her other patients.

She did not have a single moment to waste thinking about Josh Calhoun.

Finally, she went to her room.

There was a bouquet of daisies and sunflowers on her coffee table.

The card read, "L—you deserve a better class of friends. J."

Now what the hell was *that* supposed to mean?

Eleven

Josh's phone rang as he was trying to make sense of the latest sales for Calhoun Creamery's new Greek yogurt line. The numbers were sagging. They might've entered this market a little too late, he was forced to conclude as he answered the phone. "This is Josh," he said, putting the call on speakerphone.

"If I ask you to come back to Chicago," Carson Newport said, "will you hate me forever? Or just for a couple of days?"

"I won't hate you," Josh told him, setting his report aside. "But I'm not coming back to Chicago." *Ever*, he mentally added.

"My sisters," Carson went on as if Josh hadn't spoken, "have decided the best way to honor the extraordinary efforts of one Dr. Lucinda Wilde is to make her the guest of honor at the gala benefit we're hosting on behalf of the new children's hospital we're building."

Josh might have groaned. He wasn't sure.

"Dr. Wilde has requested that some funds raised at this benefit go to a new cardiac cath lab, seeing as we've already paid for the cancer pavilion expansion," Carson added.

This was a trap. Josh could feel it. The question was, what kind of trap was it? He hadn't figured Lucy to go cry on anyone's shoulder. She hadn't even cried on his shoulder. Of course, she hadn't punched him, either—and he certainly deserved a good walloping.

This was a huge mess and, apparently, it wasn't a mess that was going to go away if he ignored it.

"So you're building a new children's hospital, funding a cancer pavilion and now a new cardiology lab? Business must be better than I thought." Of course, Lucy would ask for something so selfless. She'd said her dad died of a heart attack, right? A less scrupulous person would have pocketed that cash or demanded a finder's fee or something.

But not his Lucy. Every single bit went right back into her hospital and her patients.

And he had called her pitiful. To her face.

"Philanthropy is good business," Carson said. "You should know that by now."

"You've neglected to mention why you're telling me this," Josh said.

"You're invited. To the benefit, that is."

Josh waited, but Carson didn't have anything else to say. "That's it? You're not going to ask me to snoop around or convince your sisters to do something for you? Has Brooks gone off the deep end? Does he need to be hauled back into reality again?"

"No," Carson said simply. "We overstepped and this is our way of making it up to you."

"If that isn't the damnedest thing I've ever heard. How do you figure that asking me to come back to Chicago is making anything up to me?"

There was a moment of silence, during which Josh's grandfather stuck his head into the office. "Everything okay?" he asked. If his grandfather had heard him, it probably meant that Josh was shouting.

Dammit. He tried to keep calm. "Carson's asking me to go to some benefit in Chicago." He hadn't exactly filled his grandfather in on the details of his disastrous trip to Chicago. And he didn't want to.

Still, his grandfather knew him too well. "Does this have something to do with our Lucy?"

"Dr. Lucinda Wilde is the guest of honor," Carson chimed in. "I think she'd want to have her friends around her. She doesn't strike me as the kind of woman who is used to a lot of media scrutiny."

Josh's grandfather gave him a warm smile. "Maybe you should go."

If Josh didn't know any better, he would have

said that the two men had planned this entire ambush. "I'm still trying to get caught up from the last time I was in Chicago," he told both of them at the same time.

"Reports will keep," his grandfather said.

"There are going to be a lot of movers and shakers at this event," Carson reminded him. "It's going to be a hell of a networking opportunity."

Josh scowled at his grandfather.

Carson, however, did not see the scowl. "Look, I was talking with Dr. Wilde the other day and she asked me to make sure you are doing okay."

"She did?" Josh said. "I mean, she asked about me?"

His grandfather cocked an eyebrow at this as Carson said, "She did. I think she was worried about you. I can't really blame her—you took off like a bat out of hell."

No one could blame her. Josh knew exactly where the blame lay—with him.

Was this his penance, then? He'd made an ass of himself with Lucy, so was he going to have to suck it up and go back to Chicago to make it up to her?

He needed to apologize to her. There was no guarantee that she would forgive him, but the guilt of how he'd treated her was eating away at him.

His grandfather said, "She was a good friend of yours," as if that was supposed to reassure Josh instead of making him feel worse.

"Well?" Carson said. "Shall I put your name down

on the guest list?" Josh's grandfather nodded encouragingly.

Josh needed to make it up to her. And he couldn't do that from Iowa. "Fine, I'll go. Send me the information I need."

"One grumpy ice-cream maker, check," Carson teased. "Anything else you need?"

Josh dropped his head into his hands and thought. He knew Lucy—or he thought he did, anyway. No, that was a cop-out. He *did* know her. And he knew that if she was going to be the guest of honor at a big gala with the movers and shakers of Chicago's high society, she'd drive herself crazy trying to decide what to wear. Because he had a feeling this was not the sort of event that she could a wear lab coat to—or even that dress she'd worn to the pizzeria.

"Yeah," he told Carson. "Can you give me your sister Nora's phone number?"

Lucy paused only long enough to drop her bag off in her room before she headed next door to see Sutton. She was, for all intents and purposes, dead on her feet. It was only Tuesday but she had worked through two weekends in a row trying to stay caught up at the hospital while keeping tabs on an increasingly grumpy Sutton Winchester. Just yesterday, she'd had to threaten to strap him down to his hospital bed to keep him from pulling out his chemo port. If love was a battlefield, this was an all-out war.

She hadn't even had time to go back to her apartment and stare helplessly at her closet. The gala was on Friday night and she was the guest of honor and she had absolutely nothing to wear. She had no idea what she was even *supposed* to wear. She had a feeling that if she showed up in the blue dress and the white cardigan she'd worn to the pizzeria with Josh—again, her thoughts went back to Josh—that John Jackson might have a stroke right then and there.

She had no time to get a dress and, frankly, at this point, she was too tired to care.

"And how are we doing…today?" she asked as she walked into Sutton's room and saw that all three Winchester daughters—Nora, Eve and Grace—were talking with Elena. That was unusual enough—she hadn't yet seen all three women in here at the same time. But the way all four women suddenly stood up straighter, wearing nearly identical fake smiles, set her nerves on edge. "Is everything okay?"

"None of these girls will bring me a rum and Coke," Sutton grumbled. "And I want a cigar."

It was official. She was in no mood to deal with his crap. "And I'd like a pony, Mr. Winchester. Sadly, neither of us is going to get what we want today." She glanced at the four women, who were staring at her like dogs eyeing a bone. "What?"

The Winchesters looked at Elena. "Dr. Wilde," Elena said in a gentle voice, and Lucy decided that maybe Elena was no longer her best work friend. "The Winchesters would like to talk to you about something. You and I can go over Sutton's vitals in a little bit."

Lucy's gaze traveled over the three Winchester sisters' faces. She knew instinctively that this was going to be yet another thing she didn't want to do and she knew she was too tired to care. "Okay, what?"

Grace Winchester was the one to step forward first. "Can we talk to you in your room?"

What would they want from her now? She shuddered to think. She wasn't going to marry anyone. She wasn't going to carry anyone's surrogate baby. She wouldn't be donating a kidney to Sutton Winchester should his suddenly decide to fail. She would not be moving into this house permanently.

Nora Winchester stepped up and slipped her arm through Lucy's. "It won't be bad," she promised as she turned Lucy around and they headed toward the open door.

"Hold out for more!" Sutton yelled behind them. For some reason, that made Nora giggle.

"Daddy!" Eve said in an exasperated tone.

Lucy was marched out of the sickroom and into her guest quarters in short order. Nora sat her down in one of the armchairs and the sisters stood around her like the three Furies. Resistance was futile. Lucy knew she was about to be assimilated. "Do I want to know?"

"We were thinking," Grace said, clapping her hands together with excitement, "that you might appreciate a little assistance in getting ready for the gala."

Lucy slumped back in the chair and stared dully at the three sisters. "Is it that obvious that I'm going to be hopeless at it?"

Eve leaned over and looked at the fading bouquet of sunflowers and daisies on the coffee table. Too late, Lucy realized she hadn't hidden the card. When Eve straightened, she had a smile on her face. It was not comforting. "Look," she said in a brisk tone, "it's our way of making it up to you. We didn't ask if you wanted to be a guest of honor at the benefit and we've been made aware of the fact that you might not have the appropriate wardrobe."

They'd "been made aware" of that? What did that mean?

But before she could formulate her thoughts into an actual question, Grace went on, "So, we're here to help!" She came over to the chair and pulled Lucy to her feet. "I love a good makeover," she said with way too much enthusiasm for Lucy's current energy levels. "A dress, obviously, plus shoes, a bag, new hair, makeup—how committed are you to those glasses?"

"There's nothing wrong with my glasses," Lucy said defensively, putting her hands up and shielding the frames on her face. At that point, she couldn't be sure that someone wouldn't whisk off her glasses, never to be seen by her again. Because she needed her glasses to find her glasses.

All three sisters exchanged looks that could only

be described as pitying. And Lucy was not having any of that. "I'm keeping my glasses and that's final," she said in her sternest voice. "And, okay—I might not have the things to wear on Friday. But I also do not have time to go clothes shopping and get my hair done and whatever it is that people do before they go to balls or galas or whatever you call them. May I remind you—again—that I am pulling down a full-time job plus caring for your father?"

"Not a problem," Grace said warmly. "Elena has already agreed to extend her shift for an extra hour or two the next couple of nights so that we can spend a little time polishing you up. We'll do it here," she said, gesturing at the room they were in.

"She seems to think it will be good for you," Nora added in a sympathetic tone. At least Lucy hoped it was sympathetic and not just pitying.

The traitor, Lucy thought. "I suppose she's getting something out of this, too?"

"She's invited, of course," Nora said. "Jenelle will be taking the shift."

Lucy sighed heavily. At least no one had asked her to donate a kidney—yet. The day wasn't over yet, though. "Do I have much of a choice?"

The three women exchanged worried looks. "If you have something you'd rather wear…" Grace started.

Lucy shook her head. "No, actually—I don't." She looked down at her boring blouse and her boring work pants and her boring shoes and the boring lab coat. Boring—that was her in a nutshell.

"And as for the cost, it's all being taken care of," Nora said. "See? I told you it wouldn't be that bad."

Lucy had the distinctive feeling that there was something she was missing about this conversation. "Fine. But I swear to all that is holy, this is the last thing I will be railroaded into on your behalf. The moment your father is stabilized, I'm going to be returning to my regularly scheduled life. Is that understood?" It wasn't much of a negotiation, but it was all she wanted at this point. Before Sutton Winchester and his various and sundry children—and Josh Calhoun—had steamrolled her life, she hadn't minded being boring. In fact, right now she missed it.

The three sisters nodded and assured her that, once they basically got done playing dress up with a real-life doll, things would be "much calmer."

Lucy let herself believe the lie simply because she was too tired to argue. Besides, getting professionally made up was almost a Cinderella dream come true.

But she was keeping her damned glasses. That was final.

Twelve

God, he hated Chicago.

Which did nothing to explain why Josh was back here for the second time in less than three weeks after having successfully managed to avoid the godforsaken city for over five years. Nor did it explain why he was climbing the steps of the Chicago Cultural Center in a tuxedo. He supposed that, at the rate he was going, he should be thankful that this wasn't where he and Sydney had gotten married. He was trying to be a better human at this point, but when faced with that sort of memory, he wasn't sure he could pull it off.

Hell, he still wasn't sure of anything as he fought the urge to yank at the bow tie around his neck and headed straight for the bar. He didn't know if it was lucky or not, but he saw that Brooks Newport was already there.

Brooks was talking to a large man in a tux that barely seemed to contain his shoulders and—if Josh didn't know any better—the man had a piece under his jacket. That was interesting. Private security or private investigator? An investigator, Josh decided. Brooks could handle his own security. Either way, the other man moved on as Josh got closer.

"Brooks."

Brooks started and turned to look at him. "I'll be damned," he said with a wide grin. "You actually showed up. I owe Graham fifty bucks." He shook Josh's hand and slapped him on the back.

"You're in a good mood," Josh said as he ordered a beer. There was no way he was getting through tonight without a shot of liquid courage. "Make any progress on your end of things?"

"Some." He took a long pull of his drink. "Get this—before he got sick, Sutton was trying to block our birth father from finding our mom, the bastard."

"And that's got you smiling?" Josh asked. He had not come back to get involved in the family drama again. He'd come back for one reason and one reason only. Still, Brooks was his friend and Josh was worried about him.

Brooks shrugged. "Because I'm going to bury Sutton Winchester if it's the last damn thing I do. His daughters thought I was doing a full-court press before?" He snorted. "They have no idea what's coming. None."

"Brooks…" Josh put a hand on his shoulder and dug deep for the thing to say that would pull his friend back from the brink of what sounded like madness. It was insane, it really was.

But Brooks looked past Josh and said, "Who is *that*? Damn. She's gorgeous."

The moment was lost. Josh followed his gaze and felt his breath catch. A stunning woman had just entered the room. She wore a dark blue gown—but it was a vibrant blue, not a conservative navy. The top of the dress was a loose-fitting satin that was wide open at the neck, revealing sloping, graceful shoulders. Her light blond hair had been arranged in delicate curls and she held a silver bag in her hand. Even at this distance, Josh could see the jewels that glittered in her ears.

The only thing he recognized was her glasses.

Otherwise, he never in a million years would have figured it was Lucy. When he'd called Nora Winchester and told her that Lucy was going to need some help getting ready for the gala, he had no idea that *this* would be the result. He'd just wanted to get her into an appropriate outfit so that she wouldn't feel overwhelmed. It'd been a selfless act. After all, Lucy was the girl who'd worn a mother-of-the-bride's dress—complete with tacky jacket—that she'd bought at a thrift store to senior prom.

He hadn't anticipated that the Winchester girls

would turn her into a goddess, though. And he especially hadn't anticipated how seeing her would affect him. His lungs quit working and his chest seized up, and regret—regret like he'd never felt before—beat him over the head with a two-by-four.

He was only vaguely aware that Brooks had shoved him forward. All he knew was that he was getting closer to Lucy as she peered around the room, her eyes large behind her glasses. She was thinking about fleeing, he realized. And then her gaze settled on him.

She took a step back. "What are you doing here?" she said, and he heard the terror in her voice.

"Apologizing," he told her. He reached over to pick up her hand and kiss the back of it. He needed to keep her from bolting. "Also, telling you how beautiful you look."

She stood stiffly as his lips brushed over her skin. "Apology accepted," she said, each syllable sounding like she was chewing on glass.

From where he was bent over her hand, he lifted his eyes until he met her gaze. "No, I don't think it is. You're still furious with me. Frankly, I'm surprised you haven't punched me yet."

"I should, you know."

"You absolutely should." He stood and smoothly tucked her hand into the crook of his arm. "You look gorgeous tonight." He began to lead her toward the bar, but he saw that Brooks had bailed. Damn that man's hide.

"Josh, please spare me. I'm already nervous. Don't make it worse than it already is."

He had opened his mouth to reassure her, when a voice called out, "Dr. Wilde!"

"It just got worse," she said in a low whisper as they turned toward the sound of the voice. Josh didn't recognize the man who was working his way through the crowd toward them, but Lucy did.

"Old boyfriend?" he whispered back.

"Later? I'm going to kill you," she muttered. Then, in a fake cheerful voice, she said, "Mr. Jackson! This appears to be quite a success thus far. The place is packed. John Jackson, this is an...old friend of mine, Josh Calhoun. Josh, this is John Jackson, the vice president of Midwest. He's been working closely with the Winchesters and the Newports to manage my time and their many generous donations."

Josh shook the man's hand. Why had he said that? Why had he risked further antagonizing Lucy, asking if this guy was a boyfriend? Later, when she killed him, he was going to deserve it. "This is quite a party," he said, which was one of those meaningless things people said at parties because somebody had to say something.

"Isn't it? I'm beginning to think that anything the Winchesters and the Newports touch turns to gold." He stepped back and gave Lucy the once-over, which make the hair on the back of Josh's neck stand up. "Including our dear Dr. Wilde. If it weren't for the glasses, I'm not sure I would've recognized you."

Josh's free hand clenched into a fist, but he should've known that Lucy didn't need him to defend her. "Don't get used to it," she said in a short voice. "This is a one-time-only event. Sutton Winchester is improving and the moment he is no longer my patient, I'm no longer going to be your dog at this dog-and-pony show. So you'd better get all the donations for that cardiac cath lab out of this that you can now. The clock is ticking."

John Jackson wilted for just a second before he rallied. "Right. Well, we can't say that you haven't done your best. Now if you'll excuse me... Keep up the good work," he said over his shoulder as he merged back into the crowd.

Josh rolled his eyes and turned to Lucy. "Vice president, huh?"

She exhaled heavily. "Just count yourself lucky I didn't tell him about the Calhoun Creamery—he'd have been all over you. Lord," she added, and Josh could hear her roll her eyes. "I can see this evening is going to be a smashing success. I need a drink."

Josh grinned at her. She hadn't pulled her hand away from his arm yet, which, given how big an ass he'd made of himself, was a hell of a good sign. "Look. We are conveniently located next to a bar. Champagne?" She scowled at him. "We are at a gala benefit, may I remind you. Champagne is the drink of choice."

"Fine."

Josh got two flutes of champagne and handed her

one. She sipped at it nervously as her eyes scanned the room. Josh did the same. He could just make out Graham Newport, tucked behind one of the alcoves in the bar, leaning in close to talk to...

Was that Eve Winchester?

But before he could get a better view, Nora Winchester made her way over to him on the arm of a tall, striking man. "Dr. Wilde," she said in her gentle voice. "You do look beautiful tonight. May I introduce my fiancé, Reid Chamberlain? Reid, this is Dr. Lucinda Wilde—she's been caring for my father. And this is Josh Calhoun, of the Calhoun Creamery. He's a friend of the Newports."

"Dr. Wilde," Chamberlain said in a deep voice. "The Winchesters have been singing your praises."

Josh didn't even have to look at Lucy to know that she was blushing. He could feel the heat pouring off her. For her sake, he hoped that she wasn't turning bright red.

"Thank you," she said in a tight voice.

Josh had been wrong earlier. Lucy might not need to be rescued from the likes of hospital administrators, but in the face of sincere compliments from handsome men, she was not as well equipped. So Josh jumped into the fray. "Where's Declan?" He turned to Chamberlain. "We tested out the hospital bed that his grandfather's using the night Dr. Wilde approved of the setup. He's a great kid."

Chamberlain didn't smile, but his eyes crinkled a little bit and he looked pleased. "He's at home with the nanny. I couldn't pass up an opportunity to take my future wife out for a night on the town like this."

Nora looked at Reid and smiled warmly, but next to Josh, Lucy giggled. It was a sound right out of the past—high-pitched to the point of squeaking, and it meant one thing only. She was panicking.

He put his hand on the small of her back, hoping that would reassure her. At the very least, it would piss her off, which would redirect all of her nervous energy toward him.

Nora looked at Lucy with concern. "I hope after your speech, you'll be able to enjoy yourself."

Lucy giggled again. "Oh, I'm sure I will be able to. This is all…wonderful."

Nora and Reid glanced at each other. No, Lucy wasn't fooling anyone at the moment. "If you'll excuse us," Nora said. "I'm looking for Eve."

"I thought I saw her over there," Josh said, pointing toward the alcove where he'd seen Graham earlier. But the space was empty now. "Or maybe not. Sorry."

Nora just smiled sweetly. "No worries. I'm sure she's somewhere. Mr. Calhoun, Dr. Wilde." With that, she and Reid Chamberlin disappeared back into the crowd.

"How are you doing?" Josh asked. It wasn't his fault that he had to step in a little closer to make himself heard over the noise.

"I didn't expect it to be this crowded," Lucy said in a small voice. And Josh could tell that she was worried about all these people staring at her.

"Just pretend that this is high school graduation and you're giving your valedictorian address again," he told her.

She shot him a mean look. "I was nervous before that, too."

"But it didn't stop you from giving a damn fine speech," he reminded her.

She took a longer drink of her champagne. "Flattery will get you exactly nowhere, Joshua Calhoun. I'm not listening to any of your apologies."

"Not even the ones I really mean?"

Her shoulders stiffened. "Perhaps we could save time if you just point out now which ones you didn't really mean?"

He set his champagne flute on the bar and stepped in closer so he could whisper in her ear. "I could apologize for asking the Winchester sisters to work their magic on you, but I wouldn't really mean it."

She inhaled sharply. "You did *what*?"

"I asked them to make sure that you would be ready for this—on my dime. But it was worth it because you are a goddess tonight. And any good goddess has her moments of wrath. So, to save time, I'll keep this simple." He inhaled deeply, giving her a chance to pull away. She didn't. "What I said was cruel and heartless and uncalled-for. It had nothing to do with you and it had everything to do with me. That's not an excuse—but it is the truth. I screwed up and I'm sorry." Her nostrils flared, but she didn't tell him off. "Now it's up to you whether you destroy me or show benevolent mercy. My fate is in your hands."

She drank the rest of her champagne, set her glass down on the bar behind him with a *thunk* and turned to him. Forgiveness was not in her eyes. "No, it's not. Now if you'll excuse me, I have a speech to give."

Lucy didn't remember giving her little speech. On a basic level, she turned on autopilot, read from her prepared notes and smiled a big fake smile for the photos. There were a *lot* of photos. Lucy was positioned between the Newports and the Winchesters. The hospital administrators also had to get their pictures taken with everyone in seemingly every permutation. Then Lucy had to stand and smile while millionaires and billionaires posed and grinned for the society pages. She was vaguely aware that these people were all writing checks to the new children's hospital and Midwest, and at one point John Jackson leaned over and whispered there was now a bidding war to see who would get to name the new cardiac cath lab. He seemed excited about this.

It *was* exciting, she supposed. So why wasn't she more excited?

Because no matter where she looked, Josh Calhoun—the bane of her existence—was there. That was bad enough, but the fact that he looked absolutely stunning in a custom-fit tuxedo? The fact that, even when he appeared to be in conversation with another beautiful woman, his eyes were always on her—as though she was the only woman in the room? As though she was a goddess, for crying out loud? It was all unbearable.

She was not a goddess. Not now, not ever.

She wanted to be so mad at him for hijacking yet another part of her life. Sure, it hadn't been that bad trying on gorgeous, expensive dresses with one or more of the Winchester sisters pointing out how good she looked in this one, how flattering the cut of that one was on her. And, no, it hadn't been the worst thing in the world to have a hairstylist and a makeup artist appear in her guest quarters to transform her into—well, into someone who still wasn't a goddess, but someone who at least fit in at this red-carpet event. And the relief of knowing that people wouldn't look at her and see a hopeless case counted for a lot, actually.

But was this an apology? Between the dress, the shoes, the jewels—yes, even the underwear—she was wearing about six thousand dollars' worth of stuff. All stuff Josh had paid for. For her. Maybe that was how millionaire business owners apologized?

But she didn't feel like herself. Not Dr. Lucinda Wilde, not Lucy Wilde. She felt like was…window dressing.

After all the speeches—and there were a lot of them—were done and the photos had all been taken, the band started up. Because what was a gala benefit ball without the dancing?

She knew what was coming and before she'd even made it four steps toward the bar, Josh Calhoun was at her side again. "You're doing great," he whispered in her ear and damn it all, it made her feel better. Because she had no way to tell if she was being gracious or professional or respectable. The whole evening was a blur of flashbulbs and microphones.

But she didn't want his reassurances. She didn't want him to make her feel better. Not when she knew that he could make her feel worse with a cutting look and a few well-placed barbs.

"Dance with me?" he asked.

Oh, lovely. A request. Not an order.

"Or do you need a drink first? I can get us some more champagne."

Us. There was no *us.*

Which did not explain why she heard herself say, "Champagne would be great."

"Don't move. I'll be right back." Then he was gone, cutting a swath through the crowd at an impressive rate of speed.

She did move, though. She took several steps back into the shadows, away from the dance floor and the people and the noise. Could she go home? And not back to the Winchester estate, either. Back to her apartment with its comfortable couch and floor-to-ceiling windows. Back to fuzzy pajamas with fluffy penguins on them and a pint of Calhoun Creamery ice cream to eat while she watched a silly movie.

"There you are," Josh said, handing her a flute of champagne. "Can you make it just a little bit longer?"

She stared at him. She didn't like how easily

he could read her right now. It felt…dangerous. "I haven't forgiven you for anything. You can stop being so nice."

Amazingly, his mouth curved up in a small smile. "Good. You're still feeling feisty. I was getting worried about you. And I think you have it backward. I fail to see how me being continually rude at this point would encourage you to forgive me. This, more than anything, is a situation that calls for niceness."

Lucy took a long, cool sip of her champagne. "Why are you here, really?"

"I came back for you."

Unexpectedly, Lucy's throat closed up and she felt dangerously close to tears. Tears, for God's sake! She was overly tired, that's all it was.

Josh took her champagne flute out of her hand and set it on a tray. "Come here," he said, leading her out onto the dance floor. "If you keep your forehead against my shoulder—yes, like that—then no one can see."

She wanted to ask, *see what*? But she knew. Her eyes were watering and her mouth was pulling down into a frown, and she wanted him to stop being so damned nice to her. She didn't want to feel as if he was trying to protect her. She didn't want to need protecting.

But the simple fact was that she was out of her league here and he—of all people—wasn't.

Even weirder was the fact that Josh Calhoun could dance. Dance! "This is new," she whispered, trying to talk around the stupid lump in her throat. "As I recall, didn't you squash the hell out of my toes at prom once?"

"I did. I also squashed the hell out of Sydney's toes before we got married. Therefore, I was subjected to several long months of dance lessons so that I would not make a fool of myself at my wedding reception. Funny," he said as he spun Lucy in a small circle. She had no idea what dance they were doing. She just let him lead her around the dance floor. "I had forgotten I knew how to dance."

She leaned against him and let him guide her. "I don't know what to do about you, Josh."

He took a deep breath and let it out slowly before he answered. "What do you mean?"

"I mean, I keep promising myself that I'm going to stop embarrassing myself with you. And I do okay with that when we're around other people. But I can't seem to be alone with you without something happening."

"Something good—or something bad?"

"Both."

They took another turn around the dance floor before he said anything else. "Help me out here. When, exactly, have you embarrassed yourself in front of me?"

"Are you serious?"

"Completely. Hang on." The next thing she knew, Lucy had been dipped down low—which meant she wasn't hiding her face against his shoulder anymore. With a look on his face that she couldn't read, Josh held her there for two heartbeats before he pulled her back into his arms and began to move around the floor again. "Because I'm pretty sure I'm the one who has been busy making a fool of himself."

"Okay, fine. If this is how you want to play it, *fine*. I didn't think I could be any more humiliated than I was when you turned me away after Gary died. And I felt like an idiot after we made out on the couch and you made it seem like that was part of your plan to get into the Winchester estate. And I am not now, nor have I ever been, a pitiful virgin." She knew she was turning bright red. "Not to mention that saying all of those things out loud to you is embarrassing all over again. And the fact that we are having this conversation in the middle of a crowded dance floor in front of the highest of Chicago's high society is not helping."

"I would have this conversation with you anywhere," he told her, and, damn him, he sounded like he meant it. "Because that's not how I remember it, Lucy. I remember making an ass of myself and hurting your feelings over and over and over again. I remember lashing out at you when what you needed was a friend. I remember being so lost in my own grief that I couldn't think about yours." He swallowed, his Adam's apple bobbing dangerously near her nose. God, he even smelled good.

"I remember failing you," he went on in a low voice. "And I'm trying so hard not to fail you again. You are the kindest, most compassionate, most intelligent person I know, and I've never understood why you put up with me." She buried her face against his shoulder, swallowing reflexively, but it didn't move the lump in her throat. He held her close and began stroking her back. "God, Lucy, don't cry. I'd rather you punched me, instead."

"I don't want to punch you," she told him, her voice cracking over the words. "I don't know what I want anymore. And what's more, I don't know what to do with you."

"Hang on again," he said, and spun Lucy out and then pulled her back into his arms. Compared to the prom where he had nearly broken every single one of her toes, this was like moving on a cloud. He must've had one hell of a dance teacher. "What do you want to do with me?" he asked when he had her back firmly in his arms.

This, she thought. Wasn't this what normal people did? Okay, so maybe not the whole gala benefit ball thing, but like Nora and Reid Chamberlain—this was a date night for them. They got dressed up, went out on the town, had some champagne…

They fell in love.

Was it wrong to want that? Was it wrong to stop thinking about her patients and cancer and malignant growth and hospitals and death, just for a little while?

Was it wrong to want to be swept off her feet? To know that, when she looked up in the middle of a crowded room, that Josh would be standing right there waiting for her? Telling her she was a goddess, that she was doing a great job?

"It's been five years since I was with another woman," Josh whispered, low and close to her ear. "I didn't want to be with anyone. I didn't want to risk the pain again. That's what I told myself. But the truth is, there hasn't been anyone else who's been worth the risk. But you are, Lucy. I made a mess of it. I had trouble reconciling the girl I used to like with the woman I'm attracted to now and I reacted poorly."

"That's one way to put it." She tried to say it ironically, but her heart was pounding too hard.

"I know I don't deserve a second chance—or even a third one," he added, leaning her back so that he could look down into her eyes. "But I didn't come here this time to keep the peace between the Newports and the Winchesters. I came to Chicago to make it up to you. So let me do that."

They'd come to a stop somewhere on the dance floor. Vaguely, she was aware that music was still playing and people were still laughing and drinking, but it didn't register. She was in the arms of a handsome man who knew her better than anyone else.

She shouldn't want this—*him*. She shouldn't crave his touch or his body. She shouldn't need him. She shouldn't feel so alone without him. She had her work and her patients and…and her work.

And it wasn't enough.

"Can we get a do-over?"

He cupped her cheek in his palm and stroked his thumb over her skin. "What do you mean?"

"A girl's first time should be special and magical. When she decides to take a lover, he should put her feelings and her pleasure first." She had no idea where these words were coming from, but they sounded good, so she kept going. She poked him in the chest. "He should whisper sweet nothings in her ear and hold her afterward. If she wants to fall asleep in her lover's arms and wake up there in the morning, then that's what she should get."

One corner of his mouth worked up into a smile. "That sounds right to me."

"I didn't get that because you 'reacted poorly.' So you owe me a night, Joshua Calhoun. I want a do-over." She poked him in the chest again. *"Now."*

His hands settled on her waist, and all she wanted to do was close her eyes and lean into him. "Can we at least go back to your place?" he asked with a sly grin.

She'd have to text Jenelle, but surely it would be okay if she didn't go back to the Winchester estate tonight. Right now, she didn't have anything else that she could give to the Newports or the Winchesters. She just needed a little time. For once, she wanted to do something for herself. "You'd better make it up to me."

Something wicked glinted in his eyes and a shiver went through her body. "I will."

Thirteen

Josh kissed her in the back of the cab, his hands cupping her face and his breath fluttering over her skin. He slung an arm around her waist and held her tight as he walked her toward the elevator in her apartment building. Once the doors closed and shut out the rest of the world, he pulled her into his arms and whispered, "I *had* to come back for you. I couldn't stay away." Then he trailed his lips over her jaw, her mouth, the hollow in her throat.

"Yes," she moaned, angling her head back to give him better access. The first time—in fact, all the other attempts—had been a mask for sadness. They had both needed the physical release so they wouldn't have to think about everything they'd lost.

But that's not what this was tonight. This wasn't about mindlessly giving herself over to pleasure. This was about actively choosing pleasure.

This was about choosing Josh and this was about Josh choosing her. Not as a substitute, not as a replacement—not to fill a void left behind by someone else.

He'd come back for her. She was worth the risk.

She had things she wanted to say, but she was too busy kissing Josh back to say them. His hands slid up the silk of her dress, caressing her body at a maddeningly slow pace. Her skin began to tingle and then burn under his touch, as if her dress had suddenly become too hot and she needed to take it off *right now*.

Somehow, they got into her apartment. It barely registered that she'd scarcely been here in weeks. All she could think about was Josh's hands on her. All she wanted to think about was this night—a night of romance. A night to feel special and wanted and—yes—irresistible.

"Tell me what you want," Josh breathed in her ear as he found her zipper and pulled it down notch by notch. "Do you want it slow and seductive or do you want it hard? You liked it hard last time, babe." She quivered at the memory. Josh exhaled against her neck and she felt his arms shake as they slid over the silk covering her breasts. "Yes, you liked it when I held you down and thrust into you and made you come, didn't you?"

"Josh," she breathed as he stroked her nipples through her dress.

"Look at you," he said in a reverential tone. "Don't hold anything back, babe. Give me all of it."

She reached back behind her to stroke the length of him through his tuxedo pants. He was hard and hot and maybe it was shameless, but she wanted him inside of her. She needed him. God, she needed him like she'd never needed anyone before in her life.

Years of sexual denial all melted away as he put his hand on the back of her neck and tilted her head forward. "I'm going to give you exactly what you want, but this time, I'm going to make sure you're ready for it." With that, he slid the dress off her shoulders and shoved it down over her hips. The expensive silk pooled at her feet and she was left in nothing but a tasteful pair of pale pink panties and a matching bra, because the Winchester sisters had had enough foresight to insist that she wear beautiful underthings with a beautiful dress. She needed to remember to send a thank-you note for that little bit of advice because listening to Josh inhale sharply as his hands stroked over her breasts and down her bottom was worth it.

"God, Lucy," he groaned, and the next thing she knew, he fell to his knees behind her and bit her bottom. Not hard, but with the feel of his teeth on her in such a hidden, intimate place, she couldn't fight the shudder that went through her.

"What are you doing?"

"Loving you," he said simply. He pulled her panties down and kissed the spot he'd bitten. Then he kissed the other side. As he did so, his hands came up between her legs and he began to stroke her.

She wasn't used to her heels and the things he was doing to her—his mouth on her, his fingers on her, his fingers *inside* of her. "I can't stand." She wasn't sure how much of it she could take. "Josh, please."

"What? 'Josh, please' what?" His fingers found her clitoris as his thumb slipped inside of her and he began to move his hand in a way that turned her brain to complete mush. "Josh, please make me come? Is that what you want to say?"

"Yes," she hissed, trying to find a way to stand that would keep her from falling over.

He bit her again, a little harder this time. Everything about Lucy's body tightened up as the climax shook her. She moaned as her knees gave, but Josh caught her. "There's my girl," he said. She couldn't help but think that he sounded a little relieved. "God, you're so beautiful when you come."

"Bed," she said weakly.

"Hmm. You can still talk. I think I need to try harder." He scooped her into his arms and stood effortlessly, as if it were the easiest thing in the world. Then he carried her to the bedroom and set her on the edge of the bed.

He got her bra undone as she worked at his pants. "Lucy—" he said through clenched teeth as she freed him from his boxer briefs and wrapped her lips around him. "What are you doing?"

"Something I've never done before," she told him as she ran her tongue up his length.

"Lucy…" he groaned. "I'm supposed to be making this up to you, not the other way around." But even as he said it, he fisted his hand in her hair—there were advantages to not always having her hair pulled back in a bun.

Maybe she wasn't doing this right—maybe she should let him be in charge. But he didn't pull her away. "You should stop." He sounded as if he was hanging on to his self-control by the very thinnest of margins.

Granted, she didn't know a lot about oral sex. Okay, so she didn't know about sex in general. So she had no idea if it was supposed to be such a turn-on to have pushed Josh to the edge like this. But it was. The space between her legs throbbed with need as she swirled her tongue around his tip and he groaned again. She knew that in a few moments he'd take back control and throw her down on this bed and do bad, bad things to her. But, right now, she was in control. And he wasn't.

His skin was smooth in her mouth—that wasn't so unexpected. But the way he tasted—that was something she hadn't anticipated. He was salty and musky and he tasted like Josh should taste. She tried to suck him into her mouth, but it didn't go quite the way she wanted it to, so she went back to licking.

"Lucy," he said, the warning in his voice clear. This time, he did pull her away from him. He bent over and kissed her hard, tangling his tongue with hers. She could feel danger in his touch. It was exciting, that danger. His teeth skimmed her lips and his hand slid between her legs, stroking her again. "You're so wet for me," he whispered into her mouth as his fingers raced across her skin.

She was buzzing with desire as Josh pulled away, pushing her down on her back and pulling her to the edge of the bed. He braced her legs under his arms. Pausing only long enough to roll on the condom, he grabbed her wrist and held it down by her side. "You let me know if this is too rough."

She couldn't stop her hips from shimmying from side to side. "I need you now," she told him, her voice shaking. "Now, Josh."

He pressed against her, his length sliding against her sex. "Impatient," he teased as she squirmed against him.

"I've been waiting decades for this," she snapped, squeezing him with her thighs and pulling him toward her. "I'm not waiting for you any longer."

Unexpectedly, he paused. "You have, haven't you?" Then he shifted his hips as he pressed against her opening. "Then I won't make you wait another second."

Lucy tensed, even though it hadn't exactly hurt last time—maybe that was the advantage of being an older virgin.

"I've got you," he said reassuringly. Then he thrust into her. There was no pain this time—just friction. Just the need to move against him, with him, as he filled her.

He was not terribly gentle. He hadn't been last time, either. She hadn't realized that it would work for her—but it did. He kept her knees trapped under his arms and held her wrists against her side and drove into her over and over again and all she had to do was lie there and let wave after wave of pleasure wash over her. She didn't have to make any life-or-death decisions. She didn't have to supervise nurses or tiptoe around administrators. Josh took care of everything.

But her orgasm danced just out of her reach until Josh let go of one of her wrists and cupped her breast. He tweaked her nipple in time with his thrusts and the shock of the sensation pushed her over the edge. She arched into his touch and moaned as her release shook her.

Josh gripped her hips and pounded into her. When he came, he made a sound that was almost animalistic. Then he withdrew, sliding down to his knees so he could rest his head against her stomach. "God, Lucy. I didn't know I could still feel this way."

She lay on her back, staring up at the ceiling, her heart pounding and her body still shaking as she tangled her fingers in his hair. Anything to touch him. "I didn't know I could feel this way at all," she admitted.

He looked up at her and grinned. "It's a good thing, I hope?"

She brushed hair out of his eyes. "It is."

"I'll be back." He had turned to go, but then paused and turned back. "And this time I'm not going to screw it up."

Lucy laughed and watched him go. He did have a damned fine butt.

She flopped back on the bed. He was getting cleaned up and then she would get cleaned up and then... And then she would go to sleep in his arms. And she would wake up there, too. And maybe in the morning, they could make love again before...

Before she had to go back to the Winchester estate. Back to being Sutton Winchester's oncologist and the head of the oncology department at Midwest.

A sense of loss invaded her happiness. She hadn't known she could feel this way—and now she did. She was discovering she liked sex and that she liked her partner to be in control. But more than that, she liked Josh. When he wasn't driving her nuts, at least. But when she went back to being Dr. Lucinda Wilde, he was going to go back to being Josh Calhoun, head of the Calhoun Creamery—based in Cedar Point, Iowa.

She shouldn't miss him. After all, they'd gone almost seventeen years without seeing each other, right? And maybe...

And maybe what? He hated Chicago and she hadn't been back to Cedar Point since after Gary's funeral. Those weren't exactly the makings of a long-distance relationship—if he even wanted one. If she even wanted one—and she didn't know if she did. It would take a lot of time away from her job and her patients.

If she wanted something more with Josh—would she be putting lives in danger?

Boy, she was overthinking this by a lot. If ever there was a situation that called for a one-day-at-a-time approach, this was it. She shouldn't be thinking about anything past breakfast tomorrow morning. Everything else could wait.

Josh came out of the bathroom and she took her turn. And then, finally, she climbed in between the sheets and curled up in Josh's arms. By some unspoken agreement, they didn't talk. That's when it all had gone wrong last time—the talking.

Instead, Josh rubbed lazy circles into her shoulder as she drifted off to sleep thinking that she was definitely going to miss *this*.

For the first time in years, Josh woke up in a woman's arms. There'd been a part of him that had been afraid of this—of being with another woman. Would he be able to fully let himself go? Or would he constantly be thinking about Sydney? The reason he hadn't started dating again was not that he was afraid he would call another woman by his wife's name, but it was still a little fear that bothered at the back of his mind.

But he knew from the moment he began to float out of sleep that it was Lucy, not Sydney, in his arms. And, honestly, he didn't know if that was a relief or something that scared him even more, because he didn't want to forget about Sydney. But he also didn't want her ghost to be between him and Lucy.

He had no idea how to honor his wife and move on with his life at the same time. But for the first time in five years, he thought he might want to try. Because he had missed this. Not just the sex—although the sex was surprisingly good. She got an *A* for effort. Enthusiasm made up for lack of experience.

Even just thinking about the way she had licked him was making him hard. Yes, enthusiasm made up for a lot.

"Humph," Lucy groaned from somewhere near his chest. She rolled onto her back and flung an arm over her forehead. She had pulled the sheets down around her waist and her breasts… God, her breasts.

Josh rolled into her and began licking her nipple. "Good morning."

"What time is it?" she mumbled. And then she moaned again. "Oh. Good morning, indeed." Her hand snaked down under the sheets and found his throbbing erection.

"A man could get used to this," he told her, shifting over her so that he covered her body with his. He was not going to insult her honor or her virtue or her work ethic. He had promised that he was going to make it up to her and he would be damned if he screwed that up.

Because this was what he wanted. Lucy was who he wanted. As he joined his body to hers, he knew that this was the only way forward for him. Lucy understood him in a way that no one else did.

Their lovemaking was quieter in the morning hours, and he was able to take his time and learn her better. He didn't have to rush anything. Somehow, they would make this work.

And when she came apart in his arms again, he let himself go and followed her over the edge. "Mine," he whispered into her hair when he fell onto her. "My beautiful Lucy."

She wrapped her arms around his chest and held him tight. "That's not too bad for a sweet nothing," she said in a shaky voice.

Something about the way she said that struck a note of fear in the back of his mind. It hadn't been what he'd expected her to say, but more than that, it was the way she said it. Aside from the shakiness, she had not sounded like a woman who had just come in his arms.

She sounded…distant, almost.

Josh levered himself up and looked down at her. Her brow was wrinkled and she had that faraway look in her eyes that meant she was thinking too hard again. "Lucy? I want to keep doing this."

A tight smile danced across her lips and then was gone. "I wish we could, but I have to work."

She put her hands on his chest and pushed him aside before she rolled out of bed.

He felt that note of fear again.

And it didn't go away when she came out of the bathroom and went to stand in front of her closet instead of coming back to bed or even smiling at him. "How much longer are you here for?"

He sat on the edge of the bed and stared at her. Where had he screwed up? There'd been no discussions of his late wife, no mention of Lucy's high school sweetheart—and he certainly hadn't accused her of being a virgin again. So why was she acting like this? "You tell me," he said in a cautious tone. "I came back for you, you know."

She tossed a nervous smile over her shoulder and then pulled out one of her basic button-up blouses. "I won't ask you to stay. I am, for the foreseeable future, still living at the Winchester estate and I know how much you hate Chicago."

That sounded final and he didn't like it. "I'm not planning on moving back here, but I thought that maybe we could…"

Lucy took a deep breath and turned to face him. Her blouse barely came to her hips and her hair was mussed, and damn it all, she was still beautiful. "I don't think we can," she told him in a carefully controlled voice, and he found himself wondering if this was what she sounded like when she talked to patients with terminal diagnoses. "This was wonderful—don't get me wrong—but I've thought about it, and I just don't think there's any way that this could be an ongoing thing."

"You what?" He couldn't believe his ears. "Lucy, don't you realize what we have?"

"It doesn't matter," she told him.

Maybe he was still asleep. Maybe this was a nightmare. He could wake up now. That would be okay. "Of course, it matters. You matter to me, Lucy."

She exhaled heavily, her shoulders slumping. "Josh, you say that now—but what happens the next time I ask a question about your wife? What happens the next time you play with a little kid and I get to watch the shadows creep into your eyes and you have to do something—anything—not to think about it until you can't avoid the truth anymore?"

"That's not what this was. Okay, maybe our first time was a little bit of that—but not this time. Damn it, Lucy. You are not just a distraction for me." The moment the words left his mouth the fear in the back of his mind blossomed into something larger. Something he could name. "And I'm not just a distraction for you—am I?"

She didn't answer right away, which was all the answer he needed. "Damn it, Lucy—I never meant to hurt you. I want to love you."

She came over to him, sorrow in her eyes. But she didn't cry. She touched his cheek and then leaned up and kissed the spot where her fingertips had warmed his skin. "I love you, too—but it doesn't change things. What happened between us…"

"It matters," he told her fiercely. "Don't you dare tell me it doesn't matter."

"It does." For the first time, he heard weakness in her voice. "But don't you understand? I was a thirty-five-year-old virgin for a reason, Josh. I am, for all intents and purposes, married to my job. I save lives. And yes—" she cut him off as he opened his mouth to argue "—part of it is that I've never had anyone I cared enough about to have a relationship with. But I do the most good fighting cancer, one patient at a time. It would be wrong to turn my back on that just because I'm in love with you. People will die if I don't do my job to the very best of my abilities."

He realized he was shaking with anger. "People die," he told her through clenched teeth. "People die all the time and there's nothing that you or I or anyone can do about it. My wife died in one of the best hospitals in Chicago because she had an aneurysm. I spent years blaming myself—*years*, Lucy. But there's nothing I could have done. There's nothing the doctors could have done. People die. Gary died. My parents died. Every day, I live in terror that my older brother Lincoln will die in whatever war-torn country he's in right now. My grandfather could die tomorrow in his sleep and be contented with his long and happy life. And there's not a goddamn thing you can do about any of it."

"You don't understand," she said, dropping her gaze and turning away from him. He caught her arm and forced her to turn back. "There *is* something I can do about it. I've spent my entire adult life doing something about it. I know I can't save Gary, but this whole thing with the Winchesters and the Newports? The children's hospital they're building? That cancer pavilion they're going to fund? Do you realize how many people that will help because I was there to take care of their father?"

"But that doesn't have to be your entire life, Lucy. You don't have to be this selfless angel. You get to have your own life, too. Just because my wife died doesn't mean I died. I'm still here. I'm still fighting. I haven't given up—and I'm sure as hell not going to give up on you. I didn't understand all those years ago why you came on to me. I didn't want to betray Gary's memory by taking his girlfriend. But turning you down and walking away from you has been one of the biggest regrets of my life and now I've got a second chance to show you how much you mean to me. I'm not going to screw that up again."

"It won't work," she said stiffly. "My job and my life are here. Your job and your life are back in Cedar Point." Her mouth twisted into a frown and he thought she might be about to cry.

Good, he thought. That stoic crap sucked.

But she didn't. Instead, she squared her shoulders and said, "Thank you for the wonderful evening— the dress and everything. Thank you for looking out for me. It's something that I hadn't realized I was missing. I accept your apology. You can go back to Iowa with a clear conscience."

He couldn't hurt any more than if she had actually punched him. "You're just going to walk away from this? From us? You don't understand how special this is. I didn't come back here because I needed a clear conscience. I came back here because I love you, damn it."

Then she cracked, just a little. "You're making this harder than it has to be," she said in a small voice.

Wasn't that rich? "That's because I'm willing to fight for what I want. And I want you."

The look she shot him was so forlorn that it cut right through him. But then she said, "It wasn't meant to be seventeen years ago and it's not meant to be now. Please, if you'll excuse me, I have to get to work. Goodbye, Josh." With that, she turned around and walked into the bathroom.

And once again Josh was all alone.

God, he hated this city.

Fourteen

Normally, on Saturdays and Sundays Lucy went down to the lakefront or did her shopping. But for the third Saturday in a row, Lucy was sitting by Sutton Winchester's bed. It wasn't as if she had to watch him every moment of the day. The treatments were working, which meant he slept a lot. Still, Lucy felt a responsibility to be here, just in case. Her nurses needed a break, anyway, and all of this time gave her the chance to review her other patient files.

Whether he realized it or not, Sutton Winchester was a test case. Inoperable cancer that had already metastasized to the lymph system was not an easy thing to treat and the fact that he was responding at all was encouraging. What worked for him might work for others, too.

Which was what was important here. Not the way her heart felt—as if it had been cut out of her chest and put in a cooler full of ice to be donated to someone else who needed it more. Not the way Josh's face had crumpled when she'd said goodbye.

Not the way she'd had one magical, romantic, *perfect* night. Her only one.

She caught herself staring at the old man. She'd seen pictures of him in his prime, of course. Sutton Winchester was hard to miss and the press had loved him. The man who was sleeping in the bed next to her workstation bore almost no resemblance to that captain of industry. She knew about his reputation— the mistresses and his willingness to get dirty when it came to business. By all accounts, Sutton Winchester was possibly the most selfish man she'd ever had the privilege to treat.

And, somehow, he was also turning out to be one of the most generous. The money that his children had donated to Midwest—in addition to the money that the Newports were already sinking into the new children's hospital—would save countless lives. As much as she did not want to personally like Sutton Winchester— and he made it very hard to like him sometimes—she couldn't help but be thankful for him.

Because of one of the most selfish, egotistical men in the world, people like Gary might have a better chance. If he'd been able to get the kind of treatment that Sutton was getting now, surely his leukemia wouldn't have killed him before he turned eighteen.

She shook her head and tried to focus on her files. She was feeling maudlin, that was all. She was tired, her feet hurt after an evening in unfamiliar high heels—and she couldn't stop thinking about Josh.

A small but insistent part of her brain was convinced she was making a mistake. A huge mistake. Because she was pretty damned sure she loved Josh.

Oh, who was she kidding? She'd loved him for years. *Years*. Even while she'd been dating Gary, she'd loved Josh. It hadn't been this passionate, intense kind of love—but even then he was a good man who protected those he cared for. He'd made a dying boy and a socially awkward girl happy simply by being himself.

And now…now he'd made her love him even more. He'd sent her flowers and brought her dinner and made love to her. Okay, yes, he'd also revealed himself to be painfully human and capable of mistakes. But everyone made mistakes. He'd made it up to her. Oh, how he had made it up to her.

But what was she supposed to do? He'd blown back into her life like a tornado—and she certainly felt destroyed. Her life was in Chicago. His was in Iowa. He couldn't stand being in Chicago because everything about it reminded him of his dead wife—and that still left open the question of children. There was no *us*, not for her and Josh. There couldn't be.

A maid delivered Lucy's lunch. There were copies of both the *Sun-Times* and the *Chicago Tribune* on the tray. Sutton roused himself and demanded to see the newspapers. Lucy handed them over without a second thought. Today's lunch was a quiche Lorraine with two slices of fresh-baked bread and delicate asparagus spears wrapped in bacon. This was not hospital food and as much as she wanted to get back to her regularly scheduled life, she was going to miss having a personal chef.

"Who is this?" Sutton said, his tone of voice demanding.

Lucy sighed and finished chewing her bite of quiche. "Who is who?"

"This is you, right? Who is this fellow you're dancing with?" Instead of holding the paper out for Lucy to see, Sutton held it up to his eyes. "My girls did a good job with you. If I were a stronger man, you'd have been dancing with me—and doing a whole lot more than dancing."

"It's good to see you're feeling better," Lucy said patiently as she set her tray aside and moved to stand next to his bed. She didn't encourage patients to hit on her—no woman in her right mind would—but it was a good sign that Sutton still had a lot of fight left in him. "Let me see." Even as she said that, she realized who had to be in the picture with her.

She'd only danced with one man. Josh Calhoun.

Sutton tilted the paper so that she could see the picture of her and Josh. Oh, God—it was a really big picture—almost half a page. The rest of the page was a write-up of the event. The entire next page of the *Sun-Times* was nothing but photos of the Newports and the Winchesters and all of the other rich and famous people who'd been there.

"Is that the fellow who keeps sending you flowers?" Sutton asked.

Lucy didn't like the way his voice had dropped and taken on a slightly suspicious tone. She paused as if she was trying to remember his name. "That's… Josh Calhoun. I think he runs the Calhoun Creamery."

That wasn't much a lie, was it? No, not really. She had conveniently failed to answer the question of whether or not Josh had been sending her flowers. It also didn't answer the question of whether or not Josh would send her any more flowers.

She didn't want him to. Was it wrong to just want a clean break?

Sutton looked as though he was thinking, so Lucy headed him off at the pass. "It was quite an event. Your daughters—and your son—did an amazing job of planning it. The hospital administrators were so happy and I think people had a really good time."

She backed away from the bed to sit down with the remains of her lunch. But she didn't have much of an appetite. She shoved the tray aside and returned her attention to her computer. Lives were on the line, after all. Her patients and their families relied upon her to be the cool, levelheaded voice of reason in a scary and dark time. She couldn't afford to be distracted by something like love.

And, really, she should be better at this. She had years of practice of holding herself apart, of keeping up a wall between her personal emotions and those of her patients. She had to—it was the only way to stay sane.

So why couldn't she keep up a wall with Josh right now?

The back of her neck prickled and she glanced over to see Sutton staring at her intently. And it was only twelve forty-five in the afternoon. How was she going to make it through the next day and a half until her nurses came back on duty without letting this grumpy old billionaire barge into her personal life?

"Yes?" Might as well get this over with. She didn't do well with dread.

"You remind me of her," Sutton said in a voice that was so quiet she almost didn't hear the words.

"Excuse me?"

His eyes drifted closed. "The look on your face… The greater good. That's what she used to say. The greater good for her sons. The greater good of my reputation. She had all these reasons why we couldn't be together…"

Lucy sat very still. What questions was she supposed to ask? Because there were questions that needed answers—she knew that. Carson Newport had been coming to visit this old man for days in the hopes that he would say something—anything— about his mother. And Sutton hadn't opened his mouth. Except to her.

Why her?

"I wish I'd fought harder," he said, his voice starting to drift. "Don't talk yourself out of what you need. She was so beautiful. You remind me of her..."

And then he was breathing deeply, his chest rising and falling.

Lucy sat there, every hair on her body standing at attention—she felt as though someone had applied the defibrillation paddles to her chest and forgotten to yell *Clear.*

The greater good? Of course, she had to be concerned with the greater good. She was a doctor. She saved lives. Everything she did was for the greater good—moving into this house, attending that gala ball. Her entire life was about the greater good. What did having her heart broken once—okay, twice—mean when held up against all of the people she had saved? It didn't mean a damned thing. What mattered was advancing cancer treatments. What mattered was comforting people during hard times in their lives. What mattered was...

What mattered was that kids like Gary died because they didn't have access to good doctors and proper treatment.

What didn't matter—what had never mattered—was that she had been a thirty-five-year-old virgin. That she had been frumpy and ugly and unable to connect with the people who surrounded her.

It didn't matter that she had been alone and that she had been lonely.

So, yes—she had her reasons. Really good reasons. And she was already fighting as hard as she could.

Somehow, Josh found himself at the cemetery where Sydney was buried. He was pleased to see that the grass was neatly mowed and there were flowers at the headstones. He'd had very little contact with his in-laws in the preceding years—they had tried to get together that next Christmas after Sydney had died, but it was too painful for all of them and they'd drifted away until it was just cards on holidays and birthdays.

"Syd, I screwed up," he told her as he knelt and pulled a stray weed away from her headstone. "I should've come to see you sooner. I'm sorry. But it just hurt too much." He sat there for a moment, waiting for the overwhelming grief he'd always felt whenever he thought about coming to visit her grave.

It didn't come. He was filled with a sense of sorrow, of regret for a life they hadn't been able to spend together—but it wasn't the crippling pain that he'd come to associate with the memory of his wife. Maybe he was finally getting over it. "I found someone," he said in a low voice. "You remember me telling you about her? Lucy. Lucy Wilde. We ran into each other again and… And there was something there. Something good. I didn't expect it and now…" He shook his head. "Now I don't know what to do. I'm the one who always knows what to do, but not this time." He scrubbed his eyes with the heels of his palms. "She says it can't work. She's married to her job and her job is here, and I can't be here because this is where you and I were. When I'm at home in Iowa, I'm okay."

Even as he said it, though, he knew that that wasn't the truth. He knew that he hadn't been okay until he came back to Chicago for Lucy. He did his job and he ran his company and he worked with his siblings—but that wasn't okay. That was just barely keeping it together.

He was so tired of keeping it together. He didn't even want to settle for being okay anymore. He wanted to feel good again.

He wanted to eat Thai food and drink wine and watch the sunset with Lucy. He wanted to take her out on the town and dance her around. He wanted to go to sleep with her in his arms and he wanted to wake up that way, too.

He swiped his eyes again. "I want to make this work with her, but I don't know how."

He didn't know how long he sat there—long enough for the back of his neck to get hot from the sun. He desperately wanted to feel Sydney's presence, to hear her voice telling him that it was going to be okay. Just as she had before the doctors had wheeled her into surgery.

But he didn't. Sydney was gone.

Josh was alone, the way he'd been for the past five years.

And if he didn't find a way to change Lucy's mind, that's how he was going to stay.

Fifteen

A week had passed since the morning Josh had realized that Lucy was not going to come out of the bathroom anytime soon and he'd gathered his clothes and walked away from her. In the seven days since, the urge to go back and force her to see reason hadn't gotten any less strong.

It was noble, really, how selfless she was. How she put her patients ahead of herself.

Josh was not that selfless. By comparison, he was a selfish, selfish person.

But more than that, he was a selfish person with a plan.

"So," his grandfather said, once Paige, Trevor and Josh's youngest sister, Rose, had all settled in the conference room at the Calhoun Creamery. "What's this all about?"

"Philanthropy," Josh told him. "I was recently reminded that philanthropy is good for business."

Paige, Trevor and Rose exchanged concerned glances, but their grandfather just smiled. "What did you have in mind?" he asked.

"I've been thinking that it's time for us to invest in the Cedar Point community more heavily. I'd like to start with the Cedar Point Regional Hospital." He took a deep breath. Sometimes, the line between selfish and selfless was so thin as to be nearly invisible. "A long time ago, my best friend died of leukemia."

Paige leaned over and placed her hand on top of his, giving him a reassuring squeeze. "Gary—I remember him."

"If he'd had a better doctor and top-notch care, the outcome might have been different." Everything might have been different. But if there was one thing he'd learned in his life, it was that there was no going back. He had to keep moving forward. "My friends, the Newports, recently donated a significant amount of money to sponsor a cancer pavilion expansion at Midwest Regional Medical Center in Chicago. Thanks to their generosity, they're going to make it one of the most advanced cancer-fighting hospitals in the country. I know we can't replicate that level of success here—but surely we can help Cedar Point Regional build a better cancer unit."

Paige and Rose exchanged another worried glance

as Trevor said, "Are you feeling all right? I mean, this is a great idea and I think we're all happy to get behind it—but you've spent the last five years hoarding the profits from the business."

Josh winced. That was true—but he hadn't thought of it like that. He had just thrown himself into the business. It hadn't been about the money. It had been about pretending to be okay. And he was done pretending.

But his grandfather was grinning widely. "I think this is a brilliant idea. But, you know, the hospital is going to need to bring in someone to run this new oncology unit. Jim Cook is a fine doctor, but I don't think he's up-to-date on the latest in cancer treatments."

Josh resisted the urge to snort with amusement. He had completely befuddled his siblings, but he wasn't fooling his grandfather. Not even a little bit. "I think I know someone who might be interested in the job." He hoped, anyway. Cedar Point Regional would never be comparable to a world-class institution like Midwest.

But people lived here. They were born here, they got married here and they died here. The best that Dr. Cook could do for most people suffering from rare forms of cancer was refer them to Des Moines to see a specialist.

Lucy was a specialist. She was one of the best. Bringing her out here was selfless because she would want to help people who didn't have any other options.

And it was 100 percent selfish because if Lucy

was in Cedar Point, saving lives and curing cancer one patient at a time, then maybe...

"It sounds like a fine idea," his grandfather declared. "You just tell us what you need us to do."

So Josh laid out his plans. He was committed. No matter what happened, the Calhoun Creamery was going to start making a difference. Paige began to formulate ideas to turn this philanthropic bent into a marketing campaign for the company. Trevor was friends with a doctor at the hospital and volunteered to make the first contact, and Rose suggested doing some limited-time flavors of ice cream with the proceeds going to the hospital fund or the American Cancer Society. Through it all, their grandfather sat there, beaming at Josh. At one point, while his siblings were busy arguing over flavors, their grandfather leaned over and said in a voice just for Josh, "I'm proud of you, son."

"I may have to make another trip to Chicago," he told his grandfather.

He clapped Josh on the back. "I think we can hold down the fort for just a little bit longer." He stood. "There always was something between you two, you know that?"

"Yeah." Now he just had to convince Lucy that that was the truth.

It was the kind of day that shook Lucy's faith. Mr. Gadhavi had died. He'd gone peacefully and his family had accepted his death—at least for the time being.

But she hated it when she lost a patient. She hated it more now because everything felt more personal than it had before…

Before Josh Calhoun had come back into her life.

She was tired. Losing a patient always took a lot out of her. It felt like a failure all over again. But on top of that, she was still living at the Winchester estate. Sutton Winchester was showing signs of, if not improving, at least holding steady. But she hadn't had a day off since the gala ball and even that hadn't been a day off. She had been professional and gracious for most of the evening. She didn't think that one dance with Josh and then coming home to make love with him and sleep in her own bed truly constituted a day off.

Part of her knew that she couldn't keep doing this. She was burning all of her candles at all ends, but she couldn't stop. People depended on her. What did being tired matter when lives were on the line?

She trudged into the Winchester mansion and stopped at her room to drop off her things before she dragged herself over to see Sutton and deal with whatever abuse he felt like dishing out today.

As she did so, Josh's words came back to her. She wanted a life back. She missed him and that was something she hadn't expected, either. She shouldn't have missed him, because she was used to not having him around. But what she wouldn't give to have dinner with him and drink a bottle of wine and make out on the couch. Or the bed.

She hadn't heard anything from him in ten days, but she'd asked for that. What had she thought would happen when she'd told him it wasn't going to work and she wasn't going to make it work? Still, the radio silence hurt.

Maybe she should take some time off. She hadn't been back to Iowa since she'd first moved into the dorms for her freshman year of college. It might be nice to go back to the one place that she considered a hometown.

And she could find Josh and...

And what? Tell him that she was tired? Tell him that she missed him? Maybe they could try to do something long-distance? It wasn't as though Iowa was on the opposite side of the planet. It probably wasn't more than a seven- or eight-hour drive. That was doable on the weekends, right?

She didn't know. She had not been kind to Josh the last time they'd seen each other. He would be well within his rights to tell her that he couldn't do long-distance and he couldn't do weekends.

She washed her face in her private bathroom and stared in the mirror. First things first. She had to get to a point where her presence here wasn't required at either the hospital or the Winchester estate every hour of the day. Then she had to get to the point where she wasn't working weekends. Once she did that...

Well, it was a start.

She headed over to see Sutton. "And how are we... today?" She came to a dead halt as she realized it was not Elena or Jenelle next to Sutton's bedside.

It was a man. And not Carson Newport, either.

Josh Calhoun was sitting next to Sutton Winchester. Even stranger, Josh had one of Sutton's thin hands in his. He appeared to be comforting the sick man.

As Lucy stood there and gaped, both men turned to look at her. And then it just got weirder because Josh smiled at her and Sutton smiled at her, as well. "There you are," Josh said. "We were waiting on you."

"We?" She realized her mouth was hanging wide open, but she was powerless to get it closed. "What are you doing here? You hate Chicago!"

"Hold out for more," Sutton said. He sounded weaker today, but then again he was smiling.

"Mr. Winchester and I were just reminiscing," Josh explained patiently. He patted the top of Sutton's hand and then stood.

"About what?" As far as Lucy knew, they'd never even met before.

"Women," Sutton croaked. "Fight harder."

For once, Lucy wished she didn't know what he was talking about. "He's right," Josh explained. "We were discussing women we've loved and lost and let go. We were discussing things we wish we'd done differently."

"Oh. That's good. Carson will be…" Josh stepped forward as Lucy's words trailed off. An unfamiliar emotion had her looking around. "Where's Elena?"

"Told her to take a break. She's been working too hard. You all have."

Sutton leaned back against his pillow and closed his eyes. "I'm tired. You guys are bothering me. Send a pretty nurse back in."

Josh raised his eyebrows at her. "I think the man needs his rest. Can I talk to you outside?"

"Hold out for more," Sutton shouted at her as Josh ushered her from the room.

"Should I even ask what he's talking about?" Josh asked as he put his hand on the small of her back. Even that small touch was enough to make her skin warm.

"Probably not. What are you doing here? And don't tell me you just came back to make nice with Sutton because Carson asked you to." She didn't know why she'd said that. It was just that she was so glad to see Josh that she couldn't think of anything else. She wanted him to be here for her. She had no right to want that, but she did.

Without even realizing it, he was directing her toward her room. They went in and he closed the door behind them. "I didn't come back because Carson asked me to," he said, and then he was cupping her face in his hands and kissing her.

And she was letting him. She was kissing him back because he was here again and she'd spent the last ten days thinking about him and trying to convince herself that she didn't want or need him. What she needed was what she'd always needed—to save lives and make people better.

She still needed that. But she needed something more.

She needed Josh.

"I missed you," she told him. "Josh, I'm so sorry. I said horrible things and I think I might've been wrong."

He leaned back against the door and grinned down at her. "You missed me?"

She could feel the heat in her cheeks. "Of course, I did. And I've been trying to figure out how I can make this work."

He lifted his eyebrows. "Come up with any solutions? I've got to tell you, I have a vested interest in the outcome." He stroked his thumbs over her cheeks and pulled her in closer.

God, it felt so good. "Cedar Point isn't that far away. We could try to do a long-distance thing. On the weekends. You wouldn't have to stay in Chicago very long, and I..."

"And you wouldn't have to give up your job," he said, tucking her head under his chin and holding her tight.

"It could work, right?" He didn't answer right away and she heard herself keep going. "I want to fight harder for you. For us. I didn't think I needed to. But I've realized that I do."

He sighed heavily and Lucy's heart almost stopped. "Long-distance could work, I suppose. But it wouldn't work for long. It wouldn't work forever. Sooner or later, we'd get tired of the drive. And I know that I would get tired of only having you in my bed once a week."

It sounded like a *no*. But he was right. A long-distance relationship like that was not a long-term solution. "Oh. Okay then."

And then he was chuckling. Actually chuckling, as if she had told a mildly amusing joke instead of admitting defeat. "I'll have you know," he told her, leaning down so he could whisper right into her ear, "that I've been trying to figure out how to make this work, too."

She looked up at him. "How? You hate Chicago and my job is here and if it's not a long-distance thing, then I don't know what it could be."

"Oh, Lucy," he said, and that definitely was not a *no*. "I would never ask you to give up your job. I know how much it means to you."

She stared at him because that also did not sound like a *yes*. "It's who I am." But even that didn't feel entirely honest, not anymore. It's who she had been. But now?

She felt as though she might be something more than just Dr. Lucinda Wilde. But she had no idea what that actually meant.

"I have a proposition for you," he said, tightening his grip on her waist.

"A proposition?" That was possibly the least romantic sounding word in the English language.

"I would never ask you to give up your job," he repeated. "But here's the funny thing—it turns out there's more than one hospital in the United States. And equally funny is the fact that many of these other hospitals also treat cancer."

She blinked at him. "So, you mean, like, get a job in Des Moines?" What the hell was he talking about? Sure, Cedar Point was a lot closer to Des Moines than it was to Chicago, but why would she relocate and essentially start her career over in a new hospital if she wasn't going to move to Cedar Point...

"Calhoun Creamery has recently decided to make an investment in the community of Cedar Point," he went on, suddenly sounding more like a CEO than a farm boy. "We're going to be endowing a fund for a brand-new cancer pavilion at Cedar Point Regional Hospital. We're still working out the details, but the hospital administrators and I agree that it would be best to bring in someone new to handle the transition. The current oncologist on staff, Dr. Jim Cook, is well into his seventies." Her eyes bugged out of her head. "It's good publicity for the creamery," he added. "I learned that from the Newports."

"Josh, what are you saying?" Because it sounded like he was saying—

"Marry me," he said. "Marry me and come home to Cedar Point and take over the oncology department at the hospital. I don't want you to give up your job. I don't want you to stop saving people and I don't want you to stop trying to beat cancer. But I do want you by my side. I want you by me today and tomorrow and for the rest of our lives. There are no guarantees in this life, Lucy, but you are worth the risk to me."

She gaped at him. Was this really happening? Because she might have collapsed in her bed and fallen asleep and had the most wonderful dream ever. *Ever.*

Josh must have taken her silence the wrong way. Instead of pulling her closer, he pushed her away, just a little bit. "I just hope that I'm worth the risk to you, too. But if I'm not, I understand."

Oh, God, she was not screwing this up. "No! I mean, yes! I mean…" She hauled him down to her and kissed him.

He stiffened in her arms, but only for a second. Then he was pulling her tight and kissing her hard.

"You're worth the risk," she told him. Giving up her job at a prestigious urban hospital and relocating to a small town in Iowa certainly was a risk.

But then, not doing either of those things was a risk, too. She'd be risking her heart and her sanity. She'd be risking a lonely life and she needed to hold out for more.

God bless Sutton Winchester, but that was exactly what she was going to do.

"Just so we're clear," Josh said with a smile. "Was that a yes or no to the marriage proposal? Because I'm not going to give up on you, Lucy."

She hiccupped, and even she didn't know if she was laughing or crying. It didn't matter because suddenly she felt right again. "Yes. Yes, I'll marry you, because I'm never going to give up on you, either."

"I love you, Dr. Lucinda Wilde."

"And I love you, Joshua Calhoun. I always have." She knew that now.

He kissed her again, harder, and in between kisses, he said, "And if I have anything to say about it, you always will."

* * * * *

Don't miss a single installment of
DYNASTIES: THE NEWPORTS
*Passion and chaos consume a Chicago
real estate empire.*

SAYING YES TO THE BOSS
by Andrea Laurence

AN HEIR FOR THE BILLIONAIRE
by Kat Cantrell

CLAIMED BY THE COWBOY
by Sarah M. Anderson

HIS SECRET BABY BOMBSHELL
by Jules Bennett

BACK IN THE ENEMY'S BED
by Michelle Celmer

THE TEXAN'S ONE NIGHT STAND-OFF
by Charlene Sands

Available now from Harlequin Desire!

***

*If you're on Twitter, tell us what you think
of Harlequin Desire! #harlequindesire*

COMING NEXT MONTH FROM

 HARLEQUIN® *Desire*

Available October 4, 2016

#2473 THE RANCHER RETURNS
The Westmoreland Legacy • by Brenda Jackson
When a Navy SEAL returns home, he finds a sexy professor digging up his ranch in search of treasure! He wants her off his land...and in his arms! But his family's secrets may stand in the way of seduction...

#2474 THE BLACK SHEEP'S SECRET CHILD
Billionaires and Babies • by Cat Schield
When his brother's widow comes to Trent Caldwell asking him to save the family company, he knows exactly what he wants in return. First, complete control of the business. Then the secretive single mother back in his bed...

#2475 THE PREGNANCY PROPOSITION
Hawaiian Nights • by Andrea Laurence
When plain Paige flies to a Hawaiian resort to fulfill her grandfather's dying wish, she's tempted by the hotel's handsome owner. Will her unplanned pregnancy ruin their chance at giving in to more than desire?

#2476 HIS SECRET BABY BOMBSHELL
Dynasties: The Newports • by Jules Bennett
After their secret affair, Graham Newport discovers Eva Winchester is pregnant! Her father is Graham's most hated business rival, but he's ready to fight for Eve and their baby...as long as he can keep his heart out of the negotiations!

#2477 CONVENIENT COWGIRL BRIDE
Red Dirt Royalty • by Silver James
Chase Barron needs a wife without pesky emotional expectations. Down-on-her-luck cowgirl Savannah Wolfe needs help getting back on the rodeo circuit. A marriage of convenience may solve both their problems—unless they fall in love...

#2478 HIS ILLEGITIMATE HEIR
The Beaumont Heirs • by Sarah M. Anderson
Zeb Richards has never wanted anything more than he wants the Beaumont's prized company. Until he meets top employee Casey Johnson. Now this boss is breaking all the rules for just one night—a night with consequences...

REQUEST YOUR FREE BOOKS!
2 FREE NOVELS PLUS 2 FREE GIFTS!

H HARLEQUIN®

Desire

ALWAYS POWERFUL, PASSIONATE AND PROVOCATIVE

YES! Please send me 2 FREE Harlequin® Desire novels and my 2 FREE gifts (gifts are worth about $10). After receiving them, if I don't wish to receive any more books, I can return the shipping statement marked "cancel." If I don't cancel, I will receive 6 brand-new novels every month and be billed just $4.55 per book in the U.S. or $5.24 per book in Canada. That's a savings of at least 13% off the cover price! It's quite a bargain! Shipping and handling is just 50¢ per book in the U.S. and 75¢ per book in Canada.* I understand that accepting the 2 free books and gifts places me under no obligation to buy anything. I can always return a shipment and cancel at any time. Even if I never buy another book, the two free books and gifts are mine to keep forever.

225/326 HDN GH2P

Name _____ (PLEASE PRINT) _____

Address _____ Apt. # _____

City _____ State/Prov. _____ Zip/Postal Code _____

Signature (if under 18, a parent or guardian must sign)

Mail to the **Reader Service**:
IN U.S.A.: P.O. Box 1867, Buffalo, NY 14240-1867
IN CANADA: P.O. Box 609, Fort Erie, Ontario L2A 5X3

Want to try two free books from another line?
Call 1-800-873-8635 or visit www.ReaderService.com.

* Terms and prices subject to change without notice. Prices do not include applicable taxes. Sales tax applicable in N.Y. Canadian residents will be charged applicable taxes. Offer not valid in Quebec. This offer is limited to one order per household. Not valid for current subscribers to Harlequin Desire books. All orders subject to credit approval. Credit or debit balances in a customer's account(s) may be offset by any other outstanding balance owed by or to the customer. Please allow 4 to 6 weeks for delivery. Offer available while quantities last.

Your Privacy—The Reader Service is committed to protecting your privacy. Our Privacy Policy is available online at www.ReaderService.com or upon request from the Reader Service.

We make a portion of our mailing list available to reputable third parties that offer products we believe may interest you. If you prefer that we not exchange your name with third parties, or if you wish to clarify or modify your communication preferences, please visit us at www.ReaderService.com/consumerschoice or write to us at Reader Service Preference Service, P.O. Box 9062, Buffalo, NY 14240-9062. Include your complete name and address.

HD15

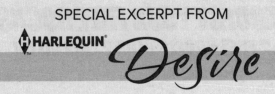
Gavin grabbed his duffel from the truck. He tilted his Stetson back on his head and looked at the car parked in front of his grandmother's guest cottage. Gavin hoped his grandmother hadn't extended an invitation for that professor to stay on their property as well as dig on their land. He didn't want anyone taking advantage of his family.

He'd taken one step onto the porch when the front door swung open and his grandmother walked out. She was smiling, and when she opened her arms, he dropped his duffel bag and walked straight into the hug awaiting him.

"Welcome home, Gavin," she said. "I didn't expect you for a few months yet. Did everything go okay?"

He smiled. She always asked him the same thing, knowing full well that because of the classified nature of his job as a SEAL, he couldn't tell her anything. "Yes, Gramma Mel, everything went okay. I'm back because—"

Whatever You're Into… Passionate Reads

Looking for more passionate reads from Harlequin®?
Fear not! Harlequin® Presents, Harlequin® Desire and
Harlequin® Blaze offer you irresistible romance stories
featuring powerful heroes.

HARLEQUIN *Presents.*

Do you want alpha males, decadent glamour and jet-set
lifestyles? Step into the sensational, sophisticated world of
Harlequin® Presents, where sinfully tempting heroes ignite a
fierce and wickedly irresistible passion!

HARLEQUIN *Desire*

Harlequin® Desire novels are powerful, passionate and
provocative contemporary romances set against a backdrop of
wealth, privilege and sweeping family saga. Alpha heroes with
a soft side meet strong-willed but vulnerable heroines amid a
dramatic world of divided loyalties, high-stakes conflict and
intense emotion.

HARLEQUIN *Blaze*

Harlequin® Blaze stories sizzle with strong heroines and
irresistible heroes playing the game of modern love and lust.
They're fun, sexy and always steamy.

Be sure to check out our full selection of books
within each series every month!

www.Harlequin.com

HPASSION2016

He blinked, not sure he was seeing straight. A woman stood in the doorway, but she wasn't just *some* woman. She had to be the most gorgeous woman he'd ever seen. Hell, she looked like everything he'd ever fantasized a woman to be, even while fully clothed in jeans and a pullover sweater.

Gavin studied her features, trying to figure out what had him spellbound. Was it the caramel-colored skin, dark chocolate eyes, dimpled cheeks, button nose or well-defined, kissable lips? Maybe every single thing.

Not waiting for his grandmother to make introductions, his mouth eased into a smile. He reached out his hand and said, "Hello, I'm Gavin."

The moment their hands touched, a jolt of desire shot through his body. Nothing like this had ever happened to him before. From the expression that flashed in her eyes, he knew she felt it, as well.

"It's nice meeting you, Gavin," she said softly. "Layla Harris."

Harris? His aroused senses suddenly screeched to a stop. Did she say *Harris*? Was Layla related to this Professor Harris? Was she part of the excavation team?

Now he had even more questions, and he was determined to get some answers.

Don't miss
THE RANCHER RETURNS
by New York Times *bestselling author Brenda Jackson,*
available October 2016 wherever
Harlequin® Desire books and ebooks are sold.

www.Harlequin.com